POTIONS AND THE PLEASANTLY POISONED

A WILLIAMS WITCH MYSTERY
BOOK ONE

ELOISE EVERHART

ALORIUM PUBLISHING

This is a work of fiction. Names, characters, places, and incidents either are the product of the author's imagination or are used fictitiously, and any resemblance to actual persons, living or dead, business establishments, events, or locales is entirely coincidental.

PB ISBN: 978-1-962759-00-7

Author: Eloise Everhart

Editors: Alyssa Hall and Stefanie Spangler-Buswell

Cover design by GetCovers

CHAPTER 1

I cursed under my breath as a deer dashed onto the road, missing my vehicle by a few inches. I slammed on the breaks. My car slid on the water and screeched to a halt as my tires found traction at the last second. The deer stood in the middle of the street, staring wide-eyed into my headlights. After almost a full minute, it darted out of the light and disappeared into the trees.

Lightning flashed overhead. The boom of thunder shook the car half a second later. Where the deer had stood was a woman lying in the roadway, her arm outstretched toward the car. Her body was still, her blond hair covering her face. My heart raced. Lightning flashed again, and she was gone. *What was that?*

Rain pounded the windshield, obscuring my view of the roadway. I squinted out the window, the wipers going a mile a minute. *Where'd she go?* I leaned forward in my seat, stretching over the steering wheel. The roadway was empty. There was no woman. No deer. Only torrential rain. I shook my head and continued on my way.

It didn't normally rain so hard in the summer. Despite Seattle's reputation for being the Rainy City, the surrounding areas were dry from June through August. This year, the heat wave stretched into September. Grass had shriveled and browned under the scorching sun. Over the past week, a storm had swept up the coast, causing rivers to overflow and damage homes.

For a claims adjuster, it wasn't the ideal time to take off work. My request for a leave of absence had been met with resistance, which had led to an argument, a screaming match, and unemployment. I'd never said the words *I quit* before. It was a first, and a capstone to a tough year. Divorced and unemployed, I was on my way to deal with my grandmother's estate. I'd hoped to arrive earlier in the day, but I'd encountered delays all the way across the state on my road trip from Spokane to Whidbey Island. I was only a few minutes away from my final destination: my grandmother's home. Or what had been her home.

It was my house now. My lips trembled, and I clamped my jaw shut. She had always been there. Her death left an aching hole inside me. But at least I would have something to remember her by. That was what people told me, anyway.

I pulled into the driveway and drove up the hill. I parked next to the front door and peered out. The rain came down harder, obscuring the house. Despite the dark, I could see its shape looming above me. It was a massive old two-story Victorian with a wraparound porch. My grandmother hadn't changed a single detail in fifty years. In the daylight, its cream walls shone in the sun.

I grabbed my duffel bag from the back seat, braced myself, and dashed out of the car. I barreled up the steps two at a time. As I ran, I counted my steps. In the few steps it took to make it under the covered porch, the rain soaked through my jacket. Wind bit into my skin, sending a shiver down my spine. I dropped my bag on the doorstep and glanced back down the stairs. In my haste, I had run straight past the stone frog hiding the key. I cursed again and bolted down the steps to grab it. My foot slipped as I tried to leap back up, sending me crashing onto the wet earth. Mud clung to my hair as I pushed myself up.

I limped up the stairs, the floorboards creaking under my feet.

Meow.

I paused midstep. *Did I hear a meow?*

I scanned the darkness, my hand raised to shield my eyes from the worst of the storm. My grandfather had been allergic to cats, so my grandparents had never had one. The closest neighbor was almost a mile away. It was a bit far for one of the Hendersons' cats to roam.

Meow.

"Here, kitty, kitty," I shouted. Wind howled through the trees and beat against the shutters, drowning out my voice.

Nothing responded. The rain continued to pour. Muddy water dripped down the side of my face, getting into my eyes. I blinked, trying to clear it.

I called out once more and held my breath, but no answer came. I shook my head and turned toward my new temporary abode. I shut the front door behind me and scurried through the house. Muddy water dripped from my clothes, forming puddles all the way from the front door through the living room, past the kitchen, and down the long hallway to the first-floor bathroom. I flicked on the light and froze in the doorway, staring at myself in the mirror over the sink. My shoulder-length brown hair clung to the sides of my face. My gray eyes were wide. I thought of the deer, its eyes wide and unblinking. A grin spread across my face, and laughter bubbled out. I doubled over, gasping for breath as I laughed. I wiped my eyes, smudging more mud across my face.

Once I got myself under control, I crossed to the sink and cleaned up. After ten minutes, I was mud-free but damp. I studied my reflection. Once I stepped back through the door,

I would be done; the moment of mirth would be over. I hovered, clinging to joy for a little longer.

The second I went back into the living room, it hit me: *She's gone.*

I trembled as I flipped the light switch and looked around. Growing up, I'd spent almost every summer in this house. It had changed little over the years. It had the same old carpet, now threadbare. A trail of mud cut across it, stark against the pale cream. Custom bookcases lined the walls, the shelves covered with the same knickknacks. Each piece was a memento: the snow globe from our Christmas trip to New York when I was seven, a carved bone from her trip to Alaska, and a large seashell from her honeymoon in Hawaii.

I moved toward the fireplace and gazed up at a photograph above the mantel. It was an old photo, taken when my mother was still around. It hadn't been a special day. We were walking through the mall to the maternity store when my grandma grabbed my hand and pulled me and my mother into a photography studio. I'd complained the whole time about how bloated I looked, but she'd insisted. Her smile was so big as she sat between my mother and me, my hand draped across her shoulder. I blinked back a tear as I touched the family photo, my fingers hovering over the image of her face.

My grandmother had been one of the few constants in my life. She was always there for me. She'd helped me pick up the pieces after my mother left. The fact I would never see her again felt unreal. I would never stay up late talking to her on the phone. She would never give me more advice on how to handle my recent divorce. She wouldn't reassure me I was doing the right thing ever again.

My throat tightened. I swallowed, pushing down the sob threatening to escape. I'd had a dream about the call days before I received it. My grandmother always said I had good intuition. I must have picked up on something. *Would things be different if I'd warned her?* I shook my head, trying to clear those thoughts from my mind. *There isn't anything she could have done to prevent a heart attack.* The thoughts still lingered. I'd dismissed the dream, and now she was gone.

The wind beat against the house, rattling the shutters and causing the wooden beams to groan. The insulation and thick layers of wood between me and the wilderness did little to muffle the sound.

I pulled myself away from the photo and wandered through the house, moving from room to room, trailing my fingers along the walls. In the hallway, the floor still creaked in the same place. The wallpaper was still the same muted yellow with faint-pink flowers poking out between intertwining vines. The color had faded, but the print was still beautiful. Every piece of furniture was the same. I paused outside the door to the rear storage room in the daylight basement. *Did she keep it the way I left it?*

I turned the handle and peered inside. Long, narrow tables lined the walls. The condenser enlarger sat on the far wall, with basins alongside for developing prints. My darkroom was still intact. I smiled.

While my job as an insurance adjuster had required me to switch to digital over the past few years, I missed shooting on film and the art of developing and printing photos. *Perhaps I'll have an excuse to take pictures for fun while I'm in town.* I peeked into the cabinets. Although old, the supplies were still good. Tucked into the back corner was my old camera. My grin widened, and I grabbed it to put in my bag.

With a smile still on my face, I closed the door and walked upstairs. On my way up, I pulled out my phone and messaged my daughter, Grace.

DANI:
I'm sure you're already in bed. Just wanted to let you know I arrived safe and sound. Hope you're having a wonderful trip with your friends! We'll have to tell each other all about our adventures when we get home.

I paused over the word *home*. *Is it still home?* After the divorce, she'd stayed with her father while I moved to a nearby apartment. We wouldn't be living together again. At least, not anytime soon. I deleted *home* and replaced it with *back*. *When we get back.*

I pushed thoughts of my small studio apartment out of my mind. The best thing to do was focus on the task at hand. I returned to my duffel bag and lugged it into the kitchen. I pulled a notebook from the side pocket and opened it to read through the list I'd written that morning. There was a lot to deal with after someone's death. My top priority was her business. My grandmother owned the local insurance agency, and her clients were counting on me to keep things moving. I scanned the list. The first item was to check her home office for active files so I could bring them by the agency in the morning. I dropped the notebook on the counter and strode through the house to her workroom.

Papers lay scattered across my grandmother's desk. I flipped through them. It was a bunch of renewals and half-processed applications. I sorted and boxed them up. Once the desktop was clear, I moved on to the drawers. Drawer by drawer, box by box, I packed everything.

I pulled open the last drawer and paused. It was empty except for a large manilla envelope. As I touched it, guilt overwhelmed me. My chest tightened, and a knot formed in my stomach. I froze with the envelope in my hand. With each passing second, the knot in my stomach grew. My throat became thick.

What's happening? I shook myself, pushing aside the guilt

as best I could. *Grief is illogical. There's no reason I should feel guilty over an envelope. It's not like there was an envelope in my dream.* I exhaled and forced myself to turn it over. Written across the front in my grandmother's familiar script was my name: *Dani.*

I gasped and dropped it. The moment the envelope left my hand, the guilt subsided. I leaned back in my chair, my heart racing.

What's wrong with me? I sat up straight and picked it up again. My hands shook as my fingers closed around it. The guilt returned, joined by the image of my grandmother tucking the envelope away. I couldn't explain how I knew, but I was certain she had placed it there only days before her death. She'd hidden the envelope there for me to find.

I ripped it open and pulled out a worn leather journal with a piece of parchment paper, folded in half, pinned to the front.

> *My Dearest Dani,*
>
> *I have had the feeling of late my days upon this earth are dwindling. It is the way of things. Everything ends eventually. I have lived my life with few regrets. The one and only thing that haunts me is what I have done to you. A deception. I can only wish you will find it in your heart to forgive me. But for over twenty years, I have lied to you.*

I couldn't read any further. My vision swam with tears. I folded the letter and slumped against the chair. With each word, the guilt and shame grew. My heart raced, and I gasped for air. I shoved the letter and journal back into the envelope, dropped it where I'd found it, and slammed the drawer. I bolted from the room, fleeing to the kitchen.

My mind whirled between widely different trains of thought. My grandmother's words lingered in my mind. *What did she lie to me about? We talked about everything. Didn't we? Also, what do I have to feel guilty about? Not telling my grandma about my dream?* I groaned and hung my head. During moments like these, when I was alone, doubt crept in. *What was she hiding?*

Tomorrow was going to be exhausting. The unexpected letter had set my nerves on edge, and I needed to relax before I could finish reading it. My duffel bag sat on the counter. I strode to it and unpacked things for the morning: oatmeal, a can of soup for lunch, and a box of chamomile tea. I put the kettle on and leaned against the kitchen counter, waiting for the water to boil.

I stood there, mulling over the feeling of guilt. It felt foreign somehow, like it came from outside of me. *How could guilt come from outside of me? No. It has to be something I did. Right? Is this about Ed? Was I too hasty in getting a divorce?*

Last year, my grandfather passed away. I'd visited him every day for a month in hospice. On the last day, his eyes cleared. He'd clutched my hand and told me not to worry because he had lived a good life with no regrets. Every day, he chose happiness. As he gripped my hand, he told me I needed to choose happiness as well. I'd thought I had, but after he passed, I reexamined my life choices. My career. My marriage.

With the gift of hindsight, I knew staying in my marriage was a mistake. I'd married a man who made grand gestures. But after I said "I do," he changed. He became someone who chose his yearly camping trip over being there for the birth of our daughter. I'd fumed but stayed. I'd chosen what was expected, what made sense. But never happiness. I hadn't chosen happiness in years. I'd waited until our daughter graduated from high school then filed the paperwork. It was never too late to choose happiness.

The kettle screeched. I took it off the stove, my movements mechanical and practiced. Every summer for years, I would visit my grandparents, and during every stay, I would make the tea.

I rested against the counter and sipped my tea. Normally, the chamomile would calm my nerves, but not today. I hunched over the cup and breathed in the tea's scent. It was woody, with a hint of apple. The smell mixed with the scents of the house. I was home. I'd finally chosen happiness.

Then why do I feel so guilty? I turned it over in my head. It felt foreign somehow. The guilt wasn't connected to Ed, the divorce, or my daughter. The guilt was tied to the letter. A letter I had not written. *What did she mean by "lied"? Am I somehow feeling her guilt?* I shook my head. *Don't be ridiculous.*

I marched back to my grandmother's office and faltered in the doorway. *How bad can it be?* I straightened, threw back my shoulders, and strode into the room.

The second I touched the letter, the guilt returned. I sat, holding the paper as the wind howled outside. Trembling began in my fingers and moved up my arms as I unfolded the page and continued to read.

> *But for over twenty years, I have lied to you.*
>
> *It was not an easy decision. For many years, I justified it by reminding myself it was your mother's request. That does not make it right. I took something from you. And now, after all this time, I don't know how to explain. I should have sat you down and talked to you face-to-face, but I could not bear the thought of your disappointment. Another regret. Cowardice.*
>
> *With no other way to say it, I will put this simply. You are a witch.*

I blinked and reread the sentence. No matter how many times I reread it, the words did not change. My grandmother believed I was a witch. I rubbed at the bridge of my nose. *Was she suffering from dementia at the end? Witches don't exist.* I sighed and continued reading.

I know, my little bird. You are most likely sitting in my office, questioning my sanity—but it is the truth. You are a witch. As were your mother and me. It is a trait which runs through our family line, from mother to daughter. Have you never stopped to wonder why your intuition is so strong? How you are always so certain when someone has lied? Or how you know, before being told, something impactful, something ground-shakingly important, has happened? The strongest gift of our family is the Sight. When focused, we can see the future. We can see the past. We can see the strands of Fate itself.

There is much more we can do. Magic is a wondrous thing, shaped by our intentions. We can make the world more beautiful. Or much, much darker. Which brings me to the theft. The violation. The hole I have given you.

Within our family, we are an ill-fated bunch, and as we come into our own, the Sight can be too much to bear. It can drive you mad. It can be painful. Deadly, even.

Do you remember when you were thirteen years old and you had a seizure? The one and only of your life? You almost died. You were comatose for almost a week. The Sight was too strong for you. So as your mother requested, I did the unthinkable and suppressed your powers.

I had almost forgotten that winter. Nightmares had plagued me for weeks. When I woke up that morning, I discovered it had snowed overnight. I rushed outside in my pajamas. I was standing in the yard when it happened. A waking nightmare. My world went dark. My mother found me half an hour later, nearly covered in snow. I slept for six days, and when I woke, I felt foggy but never had a bad dream again. *Was it a good thing? I always thought it was. Oh, Grandma. Why didn't you ever tell me about this in person?*

A single tear dropped onto the page. I stared up at the ceiling, blinking until my eyes were dry. I shook myself and continued.

Now that I am gone, however, those powers will return.

My heart skipped a beat. I reread the line. *What does that mean? Are the nightmares coming back? Is she telling me I'm going to die?* I leaned forward and gripped the page.

I did what we thought was best, but what is best and what is right are not always the same thing. The coming days may scare you. They may be dangerous. And for that, I am sorry.

I have written down everything I have learned. Inside this journal are some simple lessons to help guide you. You are strong, and while I am sorry to burden you with this, I know you will find your footing. In time, I hope you can learn to forgive me.

With my eternal love,
Gran

I leaned back in the chair. *A witch?* A minute ago, the notion was laughable, but my grandmother's words settled inside me and felt true. Before I'd gone into labor, I'd known Ed wouldn't be there. I'd known my grandmother was dead before anyone called me. I'd known.

I wasn't sure how to feel. Rage fought with understanding. As a mother, I would do anything to keep my daughter safe. *But am I safer? Didn't this kick the problem down the road, and now I have to deal with it on my own?*

I turned it over in my mind repeatedly. Best and right. It was both and neither at the same time. I squeezed my eyes shut and whispered to myself, "They loved me. This was done out of love." I repeated it to myself a few times until the rage subsided.

The wind slammed into the side of the house, shaking the windows. A latch rattled, and the window blew open. Rainwater hit the desk. Cursing, I surged up from the seat and slammed the window shut.

Meow.

I paused, the latch of the window still between my fingers. The wind pushed against it, trying to pry the window from my grip. That sound again. It was a definite meow. Its source was hard to pinpoint. It was near the house, but I couldn't tell if it was next to the house or if the wind had carried the sound. I peered outside. The rain hadn't let up since I'd arrived. I could only see a few feet away from the house. The tree line was dark.

Meow.

I dropped the bundle back into the drawer and returned to the kitchen to grab my jacket. It was still damp from my mad dash inside. I shrugged into it and stepped out onto the porch. I stood still, straining my ears to listen. The wind blew against my face. I shuddered, thinking about the damage a storm like this could do—then paused. I didn't have to worry about it.

I giggled. It was the first time in a long time I didn't have to worry about it. I was unemployed. I wouldn't have to climb up onto the roof or crawl under a house to check for damage. It wasn't my job anymore.

The giggle stopped as I realized how much I would miss my job. Being an insurance adjuster had been my life for the past eighteen years. *What would I do next?*

Meow.

I turned toward the sound and trudged around the side of the house. The wraparound porch provided limited protection from the wind. As I moved, the meowing became louder and more insistent. I paused outside the office window. I squinted against the rain. Knowing my luck, the cat was hiding out in the trees. I bit my lip, pulled my jacket up over my head, and dashed out into the night.

I stumbled forward, my eyes searching the ground and tree line, uncertain for what I was looking for. *Something cat shaped? Would I be able to tell in the dark?*

"Here, kitty, kitty," I said, hoping it would come find me instead.

The meowing continued. I closed my eyes and tried to pinpoint the sound. The howling wind made it difficult. It came and went in bursts, the wind carrying the noise away. The rain muffled everything. I called out again, and it meowed in reply.

The sound seemed to be coming from the house. I chuckled and turned back, my eyes sweeping the ground. Right next to the stairs was a small white spot I mistook for a plant. I looked past it and tracked backward as it moved. I inched closer, my eyes trained on the white spot. "Psst, psst, psst."

It meowed in return. I jogged back to it and crouched by the porch. A white face with large blue eyes glowered at me from under the overhang. Its fur was soaked and clung to its small body. A large puddle had formed around the cat. The poor creature paced frantically around a small island in the mess, meowling as the water rose around it.

"Well, come on out, then," I said. The cat turned and circled the spot. That was when I noticed the kittens. They were tiny; their eyes hadn't opened yet.

My knees rested in the mud as I crouched. Mudwater soaked through my jeans. I would need to take a shower anyway, so I shrugged off my jacket and laid it down in front of me.

"It's okay," I whispered. I inched forward, pushing my jacket toward the cat. "You can all come inside, I promise."

I held my hand out toward her, letting her sniff my fingers. Her pale-blue eyes flicked between me, the jacket, and the stormy night sky.

"It's warm and dry inside."

She inched forward and ducked her head under my hand. I scratched her behind her ears. Her fur was slick from the rain but still soft. Under the thick layer of fur, her ribs were covered by a thin layer of muscle.

Rain poured down my spine, making me shiver. Despite the warm night, the wind made it much colder. "See? I'm not so bad. I have a can of tuna you can eat."

I continued to pet the cat for another moment, my hand moving farther and farther down her body. Once she was used to me petting all the way to her tail, I lifted her and sat her down on my jacket. She tried to dart back toward the porch, but I held her steady in one hand as I collected the kittens with the other. I piled kitten after kitten into my jacket. There were six in total. The last one was so small, it fit in the palm of my hand. I searched around to make sure I had them all. They were all there.

I bundled them in the jacket and scurried inside. I held them to my chest, the kittens squirming around in the jacket, until I got them into the mudroom and deposited them in the utility sink. Mud clung to their paws. They meowed and thrashed about, leaving trails of dirt behind them. I murmured to them as I emptied a cardboard box and lined it with some spare sheets. I dried them off as best I could and dropped them one by one into the box; the mother was last.

"You must be hungry, girl," I said, stroking her on her head as she settled in.

She headbutted my hand and purred.

Growing up, I had a dog but never a cat. I wasn't sure what to do with one. *Does she belong to someone?* She didn't have a collar.

As I located the can of tuna, I decided I would take her by the vet in the morning to check for a chip. She wolfed down the food. Once she was done, she curled up on her side. The kittens piled up against her. I watched her for a few minutes before I got up to take a shower. If I were going to stay in town longer, I would have hoped she didn't have an owner. I'd always wanted a cat. But I was only going to be here for a few weeks. Then I would be back in Spokane, living my old life, and the apartment lease didn't allow pets.

I settled into bed. *If what my grandmother wrote in her letter is true, will I ever be able to return to my old life? What does it mean to be a witch?* I tossed and turned all night, unable to sleep.

CHAPTER 2

I hadn't been to downtown Point Pleasant in a few years. It was still early. Seagulls screeched at each other as they soared over the waves in pursuit of breakfast. Clouds drifted across the sky, with narrow rays of sunshine peeking out the edges. The light reflected off the ocean and mingled with the wisps of fog along the shore, giving the beach an almost dreamlike quality.

As I strolled down Marine View Drive, a box of cats in my arms, I glanced around. While there were a few new additions, deserted storefronts that used to house local establishments like Howard's Home Video, Seaside Books, and Anthony's Fireside Pizzeria outnumbered them. My eyes lingered on the darkened windows. I'd spent my summers throughout high school chowing down on pizza at Anthony's and dashing to the pier to play at the arcade when the weather got too muggy in the evenings to be outside. While there were more darkened windows than I would like, compared to the ever-shifting landscape of downtown Spokane, it had hardly changed. There were the same grocers and pharmacies, and the same crab shack was suspended over the water at the pier. The historic downtown was clinging to life. It comforted me how many things could stay the same as my life morphed and changed.

I came to a stop on the sidewalk in front of the agency doors. It was in a two-story red-brick building with a large windowed lobby it shared with what used to be a lawyer's office. The windows to the law firm were now dark and empty.

I carefully sat the box of cats down outside the door and unlocked it. I fiddled with the door, trying to get it to stay open as I struggled to fit the box through the opening. The door swung closed before I got the box all the way through, causing the cardboard edge to wedged between the door and the frame. I cursed under my breath and shoved my shoulder against the door to wedge it back open.

"Morning, Dani," a woman behind me said. "You need help with that?"

I glanced over my shoulder at Olivia as she waddled toward the front door. Her pregnant belly was huge on her normally petite frame. I remembered my own last trimester clearly. The pregnancy had sapped my energy, but no matter how tired I got, I still couldn't sleep. I could never find a comfortable position.

Despite all that, Olivia was put-together and fashionable. Her black hair, styled in thick braids twisted together, spilled over her shoulders. It was stark against her bright-orange blouse.

"I've got it. I think." Shifting the box, I tried to enter from a different angle.

She held the door open for me, and once we were through, she grabbed the box from me and carried it around the reception desk and to the break room in the back. I objected lightly, but over the many years we had known each other, she had always been as stubborn as I was. It was a common trait among insurance professionals and one I'd recognized in her immediately when she became my gran's newest intern almost nineteen years ago. She'd worked her way up to an agent, and for the last eight years, she'd been my grandmother's business partner.

"What do you have in here? I swear the box is moving," she said as she sat it down on the table.

"Cats."

"Cats?" She raised an eyebrow.

I lifted the lid of the box, revealing the mother and her six kittens. The mother didn't have a chip, but she was so friendly, she obviously belonged to someone—or at least, she had. The vet had explained that sadly, it was not uncommon for cats to get lost or abandoned. It was heartbreaking to think someone had left her.

"Cats!" Olivia squealed. It was a note of pure joy. She reached forward, holding out her hand so the mom could sniff at her fingers.

In the morning light, the mother's subtle coloration caught my eye. In the dark, her white fur was all that stood out. But now, under the warm office lights, the caramel swirl across her back showed up. On her chest was a darker gray spot in the shape of a five-pointed star. Her kittens were almost identical to her, right down to her big blue eyes.

"Wait. Why do you have cats?"

"When I got in last night, I heard her crying under the porch. With all the rain, I couldn't leave them there."

Olivia nodded.

"I'm not sure what I'm going to do with them yet…"

"Well, they can hang out here with us for the day, and then we'll figure it out. Oh, look at that face." She stroked the mother's head. "She looks like a Star to me."

"Yeah," I said, nodding. "She does." *Did we just name her?*

Star trusted us to pick up and hold her babies. Their fur was soft. After a few minutes of cooing over them, we put them down. They immediately curled up next to their mom and nuzzled against her, seeking milk.

Olivia wouldn't let me carry the boxes in by myself. We lugged box after box into the office, stacking them on my grandmother's desk. Her workstation was almost as cluttered as her home office. I scowled at the pile and rubbed my forehead. "This is more than I expected."

Olivia squeezed my shoulder as we stood in silence, staring at the stack. "One task at a time. What's next?"

I pulled my notepad from my pocket and flipped it open. I scratched off the tasks I had already completed. *Pack up the home office*: done. *Move files to the agency*: done. My eyes lingered over the note I'd added to the bottom of the list this morning. *Search agency for anything odd.* I cleared my throat and read off the next line. "Take inventory of her client list."

She nodded. "I can do that."

"You sure?"

"Let me help. It will take me a day to catalog everything. Do you know what you're going to do with her client list when I'm done?" She held her breath, waiting for my answer.

"Probably sell it to you. You've worked together for years. You're, like, her prodigy. It would feel wrong to let anyone else buy it."

Olivia exhaled and smiled, releasing the tension hovering in the air. "That's great." She chuckled. "Although I doubt I'll stop fretting until I know what's happening with the building."

"The building?" I blinked at her.

She gestured to the surrounding space. "The building."

I read through my list again. It wasn't on there. I had forgotten my grandmother owned it. She'd left everything to me in her will; the building was mine now.

"It's going on the list." I jotted down, *Decide what to do with the building*, and flipped the notebook closed.

Olivia winced and exhaled sharply. She put her hand on her stomach as she perched on the edge of the desk.

"You okay?" I asked.

"Yeah. Little guy is kicking up a storm today." She shifted on her feet, trying to find a comfortable position as she rubbed her hand against her belly.

"When are you due?" I asked.

"Tomorrow." She smiled sheepishly.

"Tomorrow?" I stared at her, wide-eyed. "What on earth are you still doing here?"

"My maternity leave was actually supposed to start today. But then..." She waved her hand. "As a first-time mother, I'm probably going to be late. So don't worry about it. I'll be fine."

I nodded. My one and only pregnancy had gone well past my due date. Grace was a stubborn child and had refused to come out until I was almost three weeks overdue. The difference, though, was I'd been twenty when I had Grace. Olivia was almost forty. Pregnancies late in life were unpredictable.

"Anyway, my mom told me walking helps. I usually go for a stroll before work in the morning. But today, it can wait. You've got so much on your plate, and I don't want to leave you hanging." She exhaled sharply again.

I placed my hand over hers and met her gaze. Over the years, I'd become practiced at comforting people. As a claims adjuster, I only really saw customers when something had gone wrong. Managing their emotions was as important as adjusting the claim. "Liv, I've got this. Don't put your life on hold on my account."

"Are you sure?"

"Positive." I held her gaze for a second longer before releasing her hand.

"I'll keep my phone on me just in case," she said as she gathered her things. "If you need anything—and I mean anything—call me. If I'm not actively in labor, I'll answer."

I nodded. "Sure thing."

"Promise?" She turned to look at me.

"Promise," I said, crossing my heart.

She smiled and dashed out the door.

I stood up and watched Olivia walk down the street. A smile spread across my face as she bustled away. I switched the sign on the door to Open and sat at my grandmother's desk. I grabbed my purse and pulled out a photo of Grace to remind me of home while I was here. We'd taken the photo at her high school graduation. She had my dark-brown hair and her father's brown eyes. They were so dark it was hard to tell where the iris ended and the pupil began. I sat her picture on the desk and placed the purple ceramic mug she'd made me for Mother's Day next to it. My hands faltered as I set the mug down. *Will Grace be a witch too?* I closed my eyes and tried to picture what the letter said. *Shoot. I should have brought it with me. Why did I leave it at home? "Mother to daughter."* She could be. But my powers had emerged when I was thirteen. Grace would be nineteen in a few months. *If she was going to be a witch, wouldn't she be one by now? And wouldn't my gran have mentioned it? Maybe I'm the last?*

The front door chimed. I peeked up from the desk. Marsha stood in the doorway. Her dirty-blond hair was slicked back into a tight bun. She wore a black pencil skirt with a red blazer over a cream blouse. Sensible kitten heels completed the ensemble. In her arms, she carried a large box filled with plastic lawn signs and rolled-up posters. She dropped it inside the front door and sashayed toward my desk, a big, rehearsed smile on her face. "As I live and breathe. Danielle Lee. Back in town after all these years. I wish it was under better circumstances. My condolences for your loss. Your gran really was special."

I smiled and stood. "Thanks. It's Williams now. Ed and I aren't together anymore."

She frowned and pulled me into a one-armed hug. "You finally tire of that slimeball?"

I laughed. "You could say that. How have you been?"

"Good. Good. Busy." She gestured to the pile of signs.

I peered at them over her shoulder. They were simple but attractive. "Vote for a Brighter Future! Vote Matthews!" was written in big, bold blue text next to a photo of Mark Matthews. His smile was the practiced grin of a lifelong politician: too big and too white, like a dentist's advertisement.

"Still acting as campaign manager for your husband, I see. Are you still running your nursery too?" I asked.

"Always." Her smile widened. It was as perfect as her husband's.

"I don't know how you find time for it all. How are the boys?"

She beamed, her eyes crinkling at the edges. "Braydon is worried about school in the fall. He's only halfway through their optional reading list and doesn't think he'll finish it all in time. I keep telling him, 'Honey, it's optional for a reason. You don't have to read all of it,' but he is bound and determined. And Caleb, he's starting at middle school. Last week, he sat me down to discuss me walking with him in the morning. He wanted to make sure I knew he could do it himself. They grow up so fast!"

I chuckled. "I remember when Grace went through that phase. But she was a little less gentle about it."

"Anyway, enough about me. How have you been?" Marsha put an emphasis on the word *you* as she reached out and touched my shoulder. She had spent too many years in sales, and it showed.

"I'm holding it together. It's stressful. I've never had to deal with something like this on my own before. To be honest, my stomach is in knots."

Marsha nodded and rummaged in her stylish black purse. It was large and packed full of the odds and ends so often needed by a mother of young kids. "I've got just the thing." She pulled out a small pouch filled with tea bags. "Ginger tea. Made from the ginger in my greenhouse. Super fresh and settles an upset stomach like that." She snapped her fingers.

"Oh. Thank you." I grabbed the offered bag and turned toward the break room. "Did you want some tea as well?"

"I'm good," Marsha said as she followed me back.

We stood there chatting while I moved around the break room. I grabbed a mug from the shelf, and a wave of fatigue hit me. It was the same as the letter. The feeling came from outside of me. But that didn't stop it from weighing me down. My eyelids fluttered. I shook my head and grabbed another mug. This mug was met with a surge of joy. I cleared my throat and tried to focus on the conversation.

Marsha gasped and took a step back.

"Is everything all right?" I asked.

"Oh gosh. Sorry. I saw something move and thought it was a rat. Is that… a kitten?" She stepped back into the doorway.

"Yes. I found them last night."

"Oh." She peered at them. "What are you planning on doing with them?"

"I'm not sure yet," I said, stirring in a teaspoon of sugar.

She leaned against the doorframe. "I heard about a shelter in Oak Harbor."

"I'll keep it in mind." I inhaled the steam. The scent of ginger was strong, warm and almost peppery. I took my first sip. Marsha was right. My stomach settled immediately.

"Actually… since I'm already here, would it be okay if I put up a poster in your window?"

I froze. Marsha's husband, Mark, was up for reelection as mayor. In the last two elections, he'd run unopposed, but this year, he was up against Steven Bishop, Olivia's father. "Oh. I'm sorry." I floundered before remembering a phrase my grandmother quoted every time these questions came up. "But as my gran always used to say, politics and religion— two things you don't bring up at Thanksgiving and two things you don't advertise to your clientele. She wouldn't have wanted posters up. I'm sorry."

Marsha smiled, but the warmth didn't reach her eyes. "Of course. Doesn't hurt to check. Have a great rest of your morning."

"You too. And thank you for the tea."

"Anytime."

I helped her with her box and watched her leave. Gran always had the best advice. Not only would it have been awkward with Olivia here, but Steven Bishop was the better of the two candidates, according to my grandmother, anyway. Mark was too old-fashioned and hadn't adapted well with the times. If the downtown had any chance of surviving, it needed someone with fresh ideas to revitalize it. This was my gran's home. She'd worked her whole life to make Point Pleasant a vibrant community. It didn't matter that she'd kept secrets from me. Not when it came to this. I couldn't do anything to jeopardize her dreams for a thriving town.

CHAPTER 3

Soon after Marsha left, Olivia returned. She barely had time to hang up her purse before a string of customers came through the door, with only a few minutes between them. Most of the long-term clients knew me. Those who didn't eyed me for a moment before the realization sank in. After chatting with Olivia, they would stop by my grandmother's desk to extend their condolences. I tried to concentrate on their words, but so many of them wanted to hand deliver their cards. With each one, someone else's emotions rocked through my body. Curiosity mixed with sadness and concern. By lunch, a sea of people had come through, and I had gotten very little done. Her workstation was still a mess of paperwork and old sticky notes, and I was on edge. There was a difference between knowing I was a witch and experiencing it.

Is there a way to turn it off? To not feel so much when I touch things? I cursed myself for leaving the journal at home.

Olivia stretched in her chair. "You look as exhausted as I feel. It isn't usually this busy. I think word got out you were in town. When were you planning on taking a break? You should probably sneak out now if you want to eat, before the next group of well-wishers descends."

I sat up. *My lunch.* I'd forgotten the can of soup on the counter this morning while I was dealing with the cats. "Shoot. I left my food at the house."

She laughed. "Have you tried the new bistro? Abby's place, Eats and Treats."

"I wouldn't call that new. She opened up shop two years ago." I chuckled.

"Anything under a decade is new in this town. Go and grab yourself something to eat."

I checked on the cats. Star had found the water dish and food bowl I left her and figured out how to use the litter box the vet gave me. She lay curled around her babies under the table, sleeping. I refilled her food. Her head jerked up at the sound of kibble hitting the dish. She yawned, stretched, and wandered over to inspect my offering. I smiled, grabbed my purse, and headed out the door.

The bad weather from the night before had passed. The skies were blue. A warm sea breeze blew across my face, bringing with it the scent of salt and sand. The tension in my shoulders eased as I strolled along the Marine View Drive toward the boardwalk. Abby's place was off the main drag. As I got closer, I could smell the sizzling bacon and melted Gruyère cheese.

I paused at the head of the street and gazed out at the pier. The water in the cove was motionless and perfectly reflected the clouds on the horizon as if it were a mirror. The view was breathtaking. I fumbled in my purse and pulled out my camera. It was the old Nikon film camera I'd found tucked away in the darkroom. I'd used it back in the day when I still took photos for fun. I snapped a few photos of the ocean. With a satisfying click, the shutter opened and closed. I rolled the film forward to the next frame as I followed a seagull with the lens. It flew down, plunging into the water. A moment later, it emerged, a large fish in its beak. I snapped a shot as it emerged and tracked the bird until it landed on a cluster of rocks jutting out of the ocean. I took a few more photos and put away my camera.

As I turned to go down the street to the bistro, an old friend from high school came out of the bank a few doors down. I hadn't seen Jessica in person for three years, but we had kept in touch online. I raised my hand to wave but stopped midmotion when a man followed her out a second later. I recognized him from the engagement photos she'd posted. He scowled as he grabbed her hand and pulled her around to face him.

They were a stark contrast. Her honey-blond hair hung between her shoulders in a low ponytail. She wore practical clothing—jeans, running shoes, and a black tank top with thick straps covering most of her shoulders. A gentle wave of dark-brown hair fell over his forehead. It almost looked messy, but it was a purposeful muss. It reminded me of the hairstyle made popular by Leonardo DiCaprio in the late nineties. He was dressed in black slacks, with loafers and a light-blue polo shirt.

They whispered to each other. Jessica gestured wildly as she spat her words. He gritted his teeth and thrust his finger into her face. She hugged her arms to her body and stepped back, shaking her head. She strode away down the street. He called after her as she disappeared around a corner. He cursed and dropped his hand. He turned on his heel and trudged toward me up the street, his head bowed. I ducked into Abby's restaurant before he saw me. Jessica had always been a very private person and would be mortified to know I'd witnessed their argument.

The bistro had its grand opening the last time I visited my gran. In the two years since, the entire place had changed. In those early days, it was all clean, simple lines. No frills. No real decorations. But now, the red enamel floor sparkled between a series of round steel tables, each with fun plastic figurines in the center. But the star of the show was the long counter, which stretched all the way across the back wall. On one side were rows of stools, and on the other was a conveyor belt filled with baked goods. Customers filled every chair at the bar.

I drooled as I watched miniature cupcakes with buttercream frosting, chocolate-covered strawberries, and brownies with a caramel drizzle slide past, only to be snapped up by a hungry patron halfway down the line. Abby's desserts were hard to resist. She had turned this hole-in-the-wall into a simple but elegant lunch spot brimming with energy.

"Abby! This place looks amazing!" I whistled as I approached the counter.

Abby grinned. "Dani! Welcome back to town. You've been missed." Her smile shifted to a frown. "Although, I wish it were for something else. How are you holding up?"

"I'll be okay. Taking things one step at a time while also frantically trying to get as much done as I can before Olivia goes out on maternity leave," I said.

"Is she going to take it? I was getting worried she would give birth in that office and just keep going." She chuckled.

"I'm sure it'll be anytime now. Although, with everything I've got to do, I am selfishly appreciating her dedication," I said, leaning against the counter.

Abigail had moved to town after I graduated from high school, but after the past few years, she had become a fixture. First with her food truck and now with her bistro. Her menu changed almost weekly, with a few favorites that stuck around. It all varied, depending on her mood, what was in season, and the catch of the day. The line had built up behind me, so we couldn't chat for long.

"So, what's the special for today?" I asked.

"It's a hot smoked-salmon chowder. It's a little on the spicy side, but the flavor is worth the heat."

I couldn't remember seeing Olivia bring anything in, so I picked her up a bowl as well. "I'll take two. To go." I peered over the counter. "And a slice of lemon cheesecake. No. Two slices of lemon cheesecake."

She nodded and packaged up the food. "Enjoy!"

Olivia's eyes lit up when I handed her a bag of food. We tore into the smoked-salmon chowder and lemon cheesecake with gusto. Abby had thrown in a complimentary roll, which was freshly baked and still warm as I ripped the bread into pieces, the crust cracking as it came apart. I used it to sop up the last of the soup. I almost licked my fingers when I was done, but I held back since I wasn't alone.

"So, what happened to the law office?" I asked, jerking my head toward the lobby door.

"They retired about a year ago. It's been empty ever since, which is a pity. I always enjoyed having someone across the way. It wasn't the same decorating for Christmas last year without someone to compete against. Erickson thought about renting it for a while. But he retired too."

"Erickson?" I opened my cheesecake container. Abby had drawn a smiley face in a lemon sauce on top. The dollop of whip cream looked like its hair.

"Yeah. He was the local independent adjuster for a while. He handled almost every auto and property claim on the island. Since he retired, all the insurance companies have to send adjusters from across the bay. Almost all of them come in on the ferry. It adds a lot of time and expense. It's a real shame. The office would have been perfect for him. But retirement called. You should take a peek in there yourself. We could always use a good adjuster closer to home."

"Oh?" I mumbled around the edges of the cake.

She opened her mouth to respond when the door chimed. I took another bite, which melted on my tongue. I did a little happy dance in my seat as I chewed.

"I think they're for you." She nodded toward the entryway.

I put down the plate and stood. I'd almost turned all the way around when someone tackled me from the side. I swayed in place, my knees buckling under the sudden embrace.

"Why didn't you tell me you were back in town?" Heather asked.

I laughed. "I just got in last night."

"And?" She pulled away, her wild mane of red hair surrounding her face. "I had to hear from Abby you were back. Abby! I'm supposed to be the first—is that a cat?"

She peered over my shoulder. I glanced behind me. The mama cat had stuck her head out the break room door to see what the sudden commotion was.

"Yeah. I found her last night under Gran's porch."

"Ah." Heather playfully swatted at me. "Even a cat gets to know before me? Can I pet her?"

"If she'll let you. She's friendly, but she might be a little overwhelmed after the day she's had. We've been calling her Star. She's a new mom."

Heather's face lit up. She darted around me and squatted down a few feet away from the cat. She made cooing noises and held out her hand for Star to sniff at her fingers.

Behind where Heather had stood was Jessica. She smiled, lighting up the room. She carried an ease around her. It was hard to feel stressed out with her around. Whatever kerfuffle she'd had with her fiancé earlier seemed to be long forgotten.

"Jessica!" I smiled.

"I'm almost as mad as Heather, but don't think that means you're getting out of a hug." She pulled me into a warm embrace.

"How have you been?" I asked, pulling back.

"Good. I've been running around like crazy. It was a busy season. I had to design a new line of furniture for an artist's loft in Seattle. How about you?" She squeezed my arm reassuringly.

"Oh. You know." I wasn't sure how to talk about everything that had happened in my life yet. The divorce. My grandmother's death. The letter. Being a witch. How overwhelming it was to feel surges of emotion when I touched things. It was increasing in frequency too. Even the plastic spoon carried a hint of concern. It was too much too soon. "It's… I'll be okay. Getting used to the new normal."

She nodded. "Your gran really was something else. I remember when I first got into carpentry—almost everyone scoffed and told me to leave the woodworking to the men. Not your gran, though. She bought me a whittling set and told me to follow my heart."

I smiled. It was easy to imagine grandmother doing that.

"In fact," she said, "I still have those knives. I hadn't used them in a few years, but when I heard the news, I dug them out of storage. I had a few pieces of scrap wood left over from a recent job and made you this." She fished around in her bag and pulled out a wooden bird carved out of holly and ebony. It had a plump head capped with black and a small white body. Along its back, she had inlaid fine lines of ebony to outline the wings. The detail on the chickadee was immaculate.

As my fingers closed around it, I had to force myself not to drop it. The emotions rolling off of it in waves were at odds with her smiling face. Dread. Fear. For a moment, I struggled to breathe. My mouth became dry. My eyes watered. I caught flashes of a woman lying on the floor, her pale outstretched hand frozen with rigor mortis. It was the woman from the roadway. *Who is she?* I couldn't see her face because it was covered by her hair.

"Are you okay?" she asked.

I gasped and blinked. The vision of the woman disappeared, and I was left staring wide-eyed at the bird. I turned it over in my hands. "I'm just... it's beautiful."

"There are kittens?" Heather squealed.

"Kittens?" Jessica peeked over my shoulder, grinned, and darted past me for a closer look.

The proud mama cat sat inside the break room door, a kitten held in her mouth. She paraded the kitten back and forth before settling it down and running back to pick up another one. My hands shook as I tucked the sculpture away. *What was that?* I forced myself to smile and joined the group.

"And you just found them?" Heather asked.

"I did. Under the porch. I took them to the vet this morning to check to see if she had a chip, but no luck."

"What are you going to do with them?" Jessica asked.

"I'm not sure yet. Marsha mentioned a local shelter."

"You can't!" Heather spun. "What if no one takes them home?"

I chuckled. "With how cute they are? I'm sure they'll be fine."

"You know," Jessica began, "when I was in Seattle over the weekend, I stopped by a cat café for a drink. If you haven't been to one, it's a place where people have coffee while hanging out with cats. They partnered with a local rescue to adopt them out. You could do something like that if you're worried about them."

Heather's eyes widened, and she looked up at me. I grinned. The thought of the cat café chased the lingering images of the vision out of my mind. A cat café would be a good draw for the town. And it was a lot more fun to think about than an unknown dead woman.

"Of course you can take them, Heather."

Her face lit up for a second then fell as she frowned. "But I don't have a suitable space for them. Where would they sleep? What would they play with?"

"I have a cat tower at my place. *Tower* might be the wrong word. *Castle*. It's a cat castle. A client asked me to build it last year. It's custom made, six stories tall." Jessica squeezed Heather's shoulder.

"That sounds amazing," Heather said.

"Yeah. The client changed their mind after I made it, so it's just been collecting dust in my garage. I would love to donate it to the cause."

"Really?" Heather asked.

"Really." Jessica nodded, smiling.

"So long as I have first petting rights when I come in," I said.

"Deal." We shook on it.

And with that, it was settled. Jessica and I helped Heather gather up the cats and transported them over to her café. The entire way, she planned a photo shoot for them, with my help of course, so she could post pictures online to make sure the mama wasn't an unchipped runaway. "And then, if no one claims them in two weeks... I'll put them up for adoption."

Heather had taken over the Bizzy Bean Café from her mother. It was on the first floor of a converted brownstone. She lived in the apartment above it. On either side were the two halves of Bee's Bed and Breakfast, still run by her mother. They shared the same large patio out back. The row had been in her family for generations.

It was warm and inviting inside. All the tables, chairs, and booths were built out of the same deep-mahogany wood as the floors. They'd decorated every nook and cranny with reds, blacks, and yellows. Their signature bee art hung over the counter.

We carried the cats through the café, past a group of curious patrons who craned their necks to see what was inside the box, to an empty storage room in the back. I set up the litter box while Jessica fiddled with the blankets to make a comfortable bed for them.

While the mama explored the room, I picked up the runt of the litter. He fit inside the palm of my hand. I gently petted his head as he snuggled into my fingers. When he tried to nuzzle, I put him down, and he tottered over to his mother.

We wandered back out into the main area, which was alive with noise. The Bizzy Bean Café had the best coffee in town. The secret was honey-processed beans. It gave the coffee a bold but naturally sweet flavor.

Jessica peered at the rear wall, where every square foot of the floor was claimed by built-in booths. The wall opposite the coffee bar was covered in local artwork. She pointed at the artwork. "I think the cat tower should fit here. The art will need to move, and I might need to make a few adjustments. Shoot. My tool belt's at home. Do you have a measuring tape somewhere?"

"No, sorry," Heather and I answered at the same time. Heather giggled as I continued. "I usually have one, but I don't have my kit with me. I'm taking a break from home inspections."

Jessica nodded and bit her lip. "It should fit. It should. I'll swing by later to take the measurements, just in case. Either way, if it needs modifying, I can do it easily enough. The castle is massive, though. I'll need help to install it when I bring it over."

"I'll help," I offered.

We chatted for a few more minutes. Jessica and I gathered up our things and headed out of the café together. I promised I would be back bright and early to set up. For the first time in days, I smiled. I faltered for a second as I remembered my grandmother and the empty house waiting for me. I pushed aside those thoughts. Gran would want me to be happy. *It's okay to be happy about a cat café,* I reminded myself as I headed back into the office to continue packing up my grandmother's desk. *It's okay to be happy. Random visions are not your responsibility. It's not like you know who the woman is anyway.*

CHAPTER 4

I doubled over and gripped my stomach. Pain shot through me, followed by a wave of nausea. I stood, stumbled away from my chair, and fell to my knees on the hard floor. My eyes rolled as I tried to take in my surroundings. Deep-ebony hardwood floors. Warm sunlight through sheer cream curtains. Gardenias blooming outside the window. A wooden coffee table. Fresh eggshell-painted baseboards.

Where am I? How did I get here?

I crawled over broken pieces of ceramic toward the kitchen and collapsed on the cool tile floor, my arm outstretched in front of me. I stared at my hand through a curtain of hair. My heart raced. I twitched and froze.

I can't move. Why can't I move?

I gasped and surged up from my bed back at my grandmother's house. My heartbeat was loud in my ears, my breath even louder. *What was that?*

I blinked into the darkness and pushed my hair out of my face. In the dim light, I could make out the edges of the room. I was in the bed I'd gone to sleep in, wrapped in sweat-drenched sheets. I threw them aside, knocking pillows and the various odds and ends that had collected on the nightstand to the floor. The wooden bird clattered against the floor and tumbled under the bed. I stood, my legs shaky beneath me.

The nightmare felt so real. The thought repeated in my head as I stumbled through the house to the bathroom. My arms trembled as I turned on the water and climbed into the shower. I sank to the floor and hugged my knees to my chest. *What was that?*

The water ran until it turned cold. I shivered under the icy water and pushed myself up from the floor. My hands shook as I twisted the faucet handle off. I dried and walked from room to room on autopilot as I got ready for the day.

This was the first nightmare I'd had since I was a child. The first nightmare since my grandmother suppressed my powers. Thoughts of the package my grandmother had left me lingered in my mind. *Did this mean something? Was this the Sight Gran talked about?* I shook my head. *There was no way it meant anything. Could it?*

The air inside was stale and stuffy. I threw on some clothes and grabbed my bag. At the front door, I stopped with my hand on the doorknob. *What if it does? My hand. I was reaching forward like the woman on the road.*

I strode back through the house to my grandmother's office, retrieved the envelope from the bottom drawer, and stuffed it into my purse.

I drove to the café first to help set up the cat tower. It was dark inside. I glanced down at my dashboard. It was two minutes before six o'clock. We were meant to meet up at six, before the café opened. I idled in front of the coffee shop, waiting for Heather and Jessica for twenty minutes before giving up and continuing on to the agency to pack up Gran's desk to pass the time.

As I pulled up, I noticed Olivia's car parked outside. Her maternity leave started yesterday, but here she was—back at work before the office opened for the day. I breathed easier. After the terrible sleep I had, I needed the company.

When I walked in, Olivia was crouched in front of the filing cabinet, rummaging through papers. She had a neat stack of files sitting next to her, each one with the same blue label.

"Aren't you supposed to be off today?" I tried to joke, but my heart wasn't in it. My voice came out half-choked.

She didn't look up as she continued to pull files from the drawer. "I know. But I woke up in the middle of the night and realized the Miller Farm policy renews in two weeks. It always takes a while to process all of their paperwork."

I slumped into my grandmother's office chair and stared up at the ceiling. "Couldn't fall back to sleep, huh?"

She nodded. "Tossed and turned, but no position was comfortable. Once I thought about all the paperwork, I couldn't stop thinking about it."

"Same. Minus Miller Farms. Although at least I can catch up on my sleep. Soon, you're going to be run ragged by the little one. I barely slept for months after Grace was born."

"Ugh. Don't remind me. I've always been a morning person, but this is extreme, even by my standards. I barely slept a wink past four a.m., so I figured I might as well be productive." She grabbed the last of the files and stood.

"I'm an early riser too. Not quite four a.m., but I'm usually up by six. If you want company, just text me. I'll bring—"

The telephone rang. We both looked at each other. It hardly ever rang before business hours. As I reached for it, my chest tightened as if a heavyweight had been placed on me. It was a familiar feeling. It was how I'd felt right before the hospital called me with news about Gran.

"Thank you for calling the Pleasant View Insurance Agency. This is Dani speaking."

"Dani?" Heather sobbed.

"What happened?" I whispered. I sank into the chair, my hands trembling. *The dream. It meant something.*

"She's dead," Heather stammered through her tears.

The word *dead* played through my mind. *No. No. No. Please be something else. Anything else.*

"Who?" My voice cracked. I didn't need her to answer, because I knew already. I knew. The dream came back to me. Closing my eyes, I mentally changed the color of the walls to subdued teal and replaced the area rug with a plush white sheepskin.

Jessica. She was always remodeling her house. I should have recognized it. Her woodworking signature was all over the living room.

"I found her this morning. She was late and didn't answer her phone, so I drove over to her place."

"Oh?" I wavered. I wanted to ask so many questions, but my words died in my mouth.

Olivia stood in front of me, studying my face. She grabbed for my hand and squeezed as a tear escaped my eyes.

Heather cried so hard, it took almost a minute for her to continue. Her words came out piecemeal between sobs. "She didn't answer. The front door wasn't locked, so I went in. She was on her kitchen floor. I thought she was playing around, but she didn't get up. It was awful. She was so cold when I touched her, Dani. I kept thinking, 'Why is she cold? I should warm her up.'"

I crumpled into the chair and curled into myself.

Olivia crouched down in front me, still holding my hand.

"How did she die?" I asked.

"I don't know. The coroner is taking her away right now. It looks like she just… died. I don't know, Dani. I can't believe she's gone." She sobbed.

"I'm so sorry, Heather. Thank you for calling. Do you need me to help call people?"

"Hold on a second. Leo's calling me back. How am I going

to tell him? He's going to be devastated. I've got to go." Heather hung up. Leonard, known as Leo to his friends, was Jessica's cousin. He was her only living relative. They'd been born three days apart and grown up together. He was like a brother to her.

"What's going on?" Olivia asked.

"Jessica's dead," I whispered.

"Oh no." She gasped and covered her mouth, staring at me, wide-eyed. "I'm so sorry, Dani. So soon after... I can pack up the desk if you need to leave."

I half shook my head and half nodded. I didn't know what I was going to do.

Jessica.

Dead.

I'd seen her yesterday. She was alive and vibrant. Tears streamed down my face. Olivia rose up on her heels and pulled me into a hug. She patted my back and whispered soothing words into my hair.

If I'd called someone when I woke up, would things be different? I gripped Olivia, gasping for breath between sobs. She squeezed me back as I cried, my body convulsing in the chair. *No. No, things wouldn't be different. She was cold when Heather found her, so she was already dead when I woke up. Was she? Can I be sure?*

I pulled back, wiped my face, and excused myself to the bathroom. Olivia watched me go, her face pinched. I closed the door and leaned against it. Shaking, I pulled my notebook from my pocket. I flipped past my to-do list to a blank page and scribbled everything I remembered about the dream. My hands trembled so badly my handwriting was sloppy and barely legible. I reread the words, searing them into my memory.

I put the pad of paper away and glared at myself in the mirror. There was a fire in my eyes as passion and rage mixed with a promise. I swore to myself if I ever had a prophetic dream again, I would call someone. Even if it was too late, I would call someone.

The rest of the morning passed in a blur. In Point Pleasant, gossip spread like a wildfire on a hot, dry, windy day. Within the hour, every person who came through the agency doors had already heard the news Jessica was gone. Numb, I went through the motions. I nodded at the appropriate times and murmured agreements about what a tragedy it was because she was so young. I almost took Olivia up on her suggestion to go home, but she'd been born and raised in the town. She was suffering too. It wouldn't have been right to leave her at a time like this.

At noon, we closed up shop so we could both grab a bite to eat. She drove straight home to spend time with her family. With nowhere else to go, I followed my feet to the café. As I walked in, Star greeted me by rubbing up against my legs and purring. My eyes welled up with tears once more. The last thing Jessica and I had discussed was the cat tower. *What's Heather going to do for the kitties now?*

Groups of people huddled around tables, speaking in hushed tones. I found Heather tucked away in the back corner of the café. Seated across from her was Leonard, Jessica's cousin. He glanced up at me as I approached the booth; his piercing blue eyes were red rimmed. He smiled weakly and nodded to invite me into their conversation.

"Dani. Heather mentioned you were in town," he said.

"Hi, Leo. How are you holding up?" I asked as I slid in next to Heather.

"I'm barely holding it together." He fiddled with a piece of torn-up napkin as he spoke. "I'm still trying to contact Richard. It's only three weeks until the wedding. He's probably off, handling something from her mile-long to-do list. I left him a voicemail this morning asking him to call me back. It didn't seem right to leave that on a message... but at the rate the word is spreading, he might find out before I reach him."

I reached across the table and placed my hand on his. "My condolences for your loss. I know how close you were to her."

He squeezed my fingers in thanks. "I hadn't seen her as much lately. Not since I moved to Seattle. It's so unreal. Knowing I'll never speak to her again."

I pulled my hand back, and we sat in silence. Over the years, I'd handled my fair share of fatality claims. Silence could be an important part of the grieving process. For many people, grief needed to be witnessed for it to be bearable. Physically being there was sometimes enough to make them feel like they weren't alone. I watched him tear the napkin into smaller and smaller pieces before balling it all up and pushing it to the side.

After a minute, Heather broke the silence. "Is there anything we can do to help?"

He blinked. "I don't know. There are so many things to do. I need to tell Richard. I have to contact the mortuary. Select caskets. Figure out what to do with her home. I haven't been there yet. What do you do when someone dies in a house? Isn't there special cleaning that needs to happen? Will they tear it up? Oh gosh. Who's going to buy it when it's half-torn up because she died inside?"

I gripped the bench beneath me and forced myself to stay still as my heartbeat quickened and my breath caught in my throat. *If I see it, I'll know for sure if it was her house I saw in my dream.*

"I can go take a look if you want," I offered.

"What?" he asked.

"I'm an insurance adjuster these days. I inspect homes for a living. If it'll help give you peace of mind, I can take a quick peek inside and let you know what to expect." I held my breath, waiting for his response.

He nodded. "That would be great, Dani. Thank you."

"I'll head over later today and call you after. She still owns the same place?" I inched forward in my seat.

"Yeah. She wouldn't have sold that house for anything. Her dad left it to her."

"Do you have keys?" I asked.

He shook his head. "She always had a spare hidden under the frog. I think it's still there."

I nodded. "Just like my gran."

He wiped his eyes and chuckled weakly. "I think half the town has one of those frogs. Remember Finn making them in art class? The first few were terrible, but then he built a mold and made a ton of them to sell. Mrs. Morrison was so mad."

"That's not the assignment!" Heather said sternly, in a poor imitation of their art teacher.

I snorted, trying to hold in the laugh.

"Art shouldn't be commercialized!" Leo said.

"He had boxes and boxes of them," I said. "I think I still have one on a shelf back home."

The table became still. It was a sad reminder of why I was here and that this was all temporary. Life moved on.

Leo looked up at me and held my gaze. "Thank you. I appreciate it. I just want to get all of this over with as quickly as possible."

It varied after death. Indecision froze a lot of families, while others purposely wanted to draw the process out because it was the only thing still connecting them to their loved one. But some, the rare minority, wanted to wrap things up as quickly as they could so they could move on with their lives. I blinked, somewhat surprised Leonard was the latter. *Everyone grieves differently,* I reminded myself.

"I understand. I'll help where I can. You can count on me," I said.

Heather nodded. "You can count on both of us."

He smiled and blinked back a tear. "Thanks. Jessica adored both of you. She would have wanted you involved."

Heather sniffed and wiped at her face. "What would you like me to work on? If you don't have a place yet, I could host the memorial service. I'm sure I could rope Abby into helping with the food."

"That's a great idea," Leo said. "Thank you."

We chatted for a few more minutes about funeral arrangements and the next steps before I left to inspect Jessica's home.

While I had inspected a lot of homes after a fatality, this would be the first where the dead body belonged to a friend. The dream replayed in my head. The pain. The crawling. The inability to move. My hand outstretched. I shook myself and forced my mind to focus on the next steps. *It won't help anyone if I break down now. I have to see if my dream was real. And then I have to check the home for damage. Leo is counting on me. Get yourself together.* I gripped the steering wheel the entire way there.

CHAPTER 5

I pulled up to Jessica's home. It was a cute blue craftsman cottage overlooking a well-manicured lawn. Flowers lined the walkway all the way from the porch to the white picket fence. Over the gate was a handcrafted archway, with vines intertwining through the wooden beams. I wiped my sweaty palms against my pants as I peered up at the house.

Cream-colored curtains swayed in the breeze in a second-floor window. Seeing them turned my mind to practical matters. While I was selfishly here to see if my dream had been of her death, I was still here to help a friend. I pulled a notepad out of my purse and jotted down, *Close and lock windows/doors*, as a quick reminder to shut everything up before I left. Rain was in the forecast for tonight.

I got out of the car and walked down the path to the house. Stopping at the steps, I looked for the stone frog. It was half-hidden behind a rosebush. Thorns scratched at my skin as I grabbed the spare key. Before unlocking the door, I pulled out my notepad again and added another note to my list. Leonard would want to switch the hidden key out for a lockbox Realtors liked to use.

I paused with my hand on the doorknob. I rested my

forehead against the wood. My pulse quickened as I replayed the dream in my head. Once I opened the door, there was no going back. *It's okay. So what if you are a witch? It changes nothing.* I tried to reassure myself. But me being a witch would change everything. It reframed my whole life. I counted backward from ten. When I reached one, I opened my eyes and pushed on the door.

I swallowed as my gaze wandered from corner to corner of the living room. It was bright and clean. The walls were painted a tasteful eggshell white, with the baseboards a slightly brighter color to accentuate the difference between them and the dark wood flooring. Throughout the room, Jessica had added wooden elements. Crown molding. Wainscoting. Custom trim around the archway to the dining room and kitchen. My eyes settled on the gardenias through the far window. It was the same as my dream.

I saw—no, *felt*—Jessica die.

I'm a witch.

I peered at the doorway to the kitchen. When I closed my eyes, I could still feel the kitchen tile floor under me. I couldn't move, and it was so cold. I took a faltering step toward the chair she'd slid from as the truth settled inside me. *I'm a witch. What does that mean? Am I the same person? How can I be?*

I gripped the edge of the chair. It was solid under my hands. Jessica had built it from a single piece of wood. She had attached plush cushions to make it comfortable. I ran my hand across the fabric. The wool was incredibly soft under my fingers. The sensation grounded me and stopped my thoughts from spiraling out of control. I bit my lip.

I am here to help a friend. Compose yourself. I can figure out what this means later. I rolled my shoulders back and shook my head to chase the last few nervous thoughts away.

With my mind clear, I looked around. It felt as if the room were waiting, almost as if Jessica had stepped out of the room. If I didn't know any better, I wouldn't have thought she'd died here.

I gritted my teeth and began the inspection of the home. While I would normally go straight to the room where it had happened, my feet refused to carry me there. I swallowed and explored the rest of the downstairs instead. I moved to the dining room first. Jessica was mid-renovation. The new flooring gleamed. Piled neatly in the corner were the baseboards. I pulled out my camera and took a few quick shots. *He'll want to reattach them before showing the home. Everything else is so perfect that I would hate to give a buyer the opportunity to claim it was a fixer-upper.*

I wandered down the hall to the bathroom and guest bedroom. Everything was neat and in its proper place. I took a few more quick photos before backtracking to the kitchen. Outside the archway, I paused. Heather had described Jessica as peaceful, but that didn't mean it wouldn't be bad. I exhaled sharply and shook myself. *You've got this.*

I turned the corner.

The kitchen was tasteful and clean. The lower cabinets were painted a deep-blue, almost-black color, and the uppers were white. All the appliances were brand-new but styled to look vintage. The white tile floor was almost pristine, with no obvious signs of bodily fluids. It would be a very simple job for a biohazard cleanup company to take care of. I let out the breath I had been holding. The last thing I saw before waking were those cabinets and that floor.

I took a quick photo of the room and kneeled in the doorway. *I don't have to go any further. I could leave. Everything is the same. What are the chances I saw something else?* I bit my lip, my hand hovering over the tile floor. *I have to be certain.*

I put my hand down. Black spots floated in my vision. My heart raced. My chest tightened until I couldn't breathe. I choked and stumbled back. I scrambled away from the kitchen and fled to the dining room. I stood gasping and blinking back tears. The pain. The fear. There was no doubt. I'd seen my friend.

Focus. There isn't anything I can do about it now. Go upstairs. Close the window, and then I can leave. I'm here for Leo. As I ascended the stairs, one of them creaked slightly. I noted it in my notepad. It would be a simple fix of screwing a board back into place.

The upper landing was painted in the same eggshell color, but the floors were carpeted. It was a plush maroon Berber-style carpet. I paused for a moment, letting my feet sink into it. I closed my eyes. It was quiet. The insulation in the home was good. It kept in the heat and kept out most of the noises from the street. I could hear some birdsong coming in through a door to my left. I opened it and went inside.

It was an office decorated with ebony-wood furniture. I crossed the room and leaned over the desk to close the window. As I turned back to the door, I noticed a bookshelf built out of the same wood as the other furniture. Each shelf brimmed with books.

I stepped up to the shelves and ran my fingers along the book spines. There were so many old classics intermixed with DIY guides, poetry, and sword-and-sorcery fantasy novels. Jessica had eclectic taste. I paused over a collection of poems and pulled it off the shelf. It was required reading in high school.

Despite us attending school in different states, the book had been on all of our summer reading lists before junior year. During our last week of summer, we'd all still had half the book left to read. In our brilliance, we'd decided it was a good idea to pile into Ed's car and drive up to Deception Pass State Park to camp for the weekend. By the light of a campfire, we sat under the stars and took turns reading the poems aloud to each other. When it was Jessica's turn, she stood, planted a foot on a large piece of driftwood, and with her arms raised, she read "I Speak Not" by Lord Byron. I sat huddled between Chris and Ed, grinning like a fool. Her voice carried over the water. By the end, a family had gathered on their porch and applauded her rendition. It was the only one I remembered in any detail when school started back up. I smiled. Jessica had always made things more fun.

I flipped the book open to read from that page. A single sheet of folded paper fell from the book. I crouched to pick it up.

I gasped as I touched it; my breath caught in my throat as flashes of emotions rolled through me. Anger mixed with disgust and fear. The fear was the strongest. My hands shook as I turned the paper over and read the words.

> *A confession will do no one any good. Do not cross me. You will regret it.*

I reread the words. I didn't know how I knew, but this note was recent. It was no more than a week old. The emotions on it were vibrant and raw.

"You will regret it"? Did Jessica cross someone? Richard? They argued the day of her death. What if it was about him threatening her? I reeled back and dashed toward the door. *The sheriff needs to see this.* I froze halfway through the doorway. *"A confession"? I can't show him this.* I stood in the doorway, the different options flitting through my mind. If I showed him this, he would think Jessica had done something wrong, and she wasn't here to defend herself. It would take less than a day for rumors to spread all over town.

I paced the room. *Maybe they don't need to see it. If someone murdered her, then that would show up in the autopsy, and they could catch the killer. Wouldn't they? She was young enough they would do an autopsy, right?*

I folded the letter, put it in my camera bag, and left the house. I locked the door behind me and stashed the key back in its hiding spot. As calmly as I could, I walked to my car. I didn't have to show them the note if they were already investigating. *Let's just make sure they have a case open.*

I climbed into the car, my whole body shaking. I closed my eyes and breathed slowly through my nose as I counted back from ten again. It was a trick I'd learned from my grandfather. Ten seconds to still the mind. Ten seconds to regain control. My hands stilled as I looked up at her house. *Let's make sure the sheriff has a case open.*

CHAPTER 6

I drove up the hill to the sheriff's office, which was housed in two run-down double-wides at the edge of town, their gray paint peeling under the sun. When the department moved there four years ago, it was supposed to be a temporary holdover until the repairs to their historic brick building downtown were complete. A massive plumbing leak had cleared out an entire floor, leaving half the building cut down to the studs. Unfortunately, the town council hadn't found the funds in the budget to complete the reconstruction, and the building was now overgrown with mold. The council remained hopeful, however, so they hadn't approved the funds to tie down the manufactured homes either. Instead, the double-wides still sat perched on blocks.

I parked in the gravel lot and walked up to the main office. A metal placard welcoming visitors to the sheriff's station hung from a hook next to the front door. It was the only thing moved from the downtown location. It was a sad reminder of the stark difference between this setup and the old offices. I stopped at the entrance and ran a quick hand through my hair to straighten any flyways before stepping inside.

The door opened into a great room converted into offices and a waiting area. Cubicle partitions hid desks along the wall to the left. Peggy, the receptionist, sat at her desk in front of the kitchen counter. A black curtain hung from the ceiling behind her, hiding most of the kitchen, now a makeshift break room, from view. Peggy had worked for the sheriff's office for as long as I could remember. The entire time, she'd had silver in her hair and wore pantsuits straight out of the sixties. It was impossible to tell how old Peggy actually was. She had looked like she was in her midforties for at least the last fifteen years.

"Welcome to the Island County Sheriff's Station. How can I help you today?" Peggy asked as she typed, her eyes never leaving her screen.

"Hey, Peggy, is the sheriff in?"

Peggy glanced up as I spoke, her red-framed glasses large on her face. She grinned, grabbed her glasses, and pulled them down. They swung from a cord around her neck as she stood and stepped around her desk. "Dani! I hadn't heard you were back in town. Welcome home. Bob has a meeting coming up in a few minutes, so I'm not sure if he's available to chat. Is it something Chris can help you with, hon?"

Chris? I almost forgot he worked here. We'd been friends in high school. He was my ex-husband's best friend all the way through college. Over the years, they'd kept in touch. He was a regular attendee at Ed's fall hunting trip. *He probably won't take anything I have to say seriously after the divorce.* "Is it going to be a long meeting? I can always wait."

Peggy glanced down at her desk and traced her finger across the calendar. "Maybe? How much time do you need?"

"Five minutes?" I gave her a hopeful smile.

"I'll ring back and see if he can squeeze you in. You want a coffee or something while you wait?"

"Yes, please."

"It's self-serve. You can grab a cup over by the coffeepot.

Just put it in the kitchen when you're done." She gestured to the small table across the way as she picked up the phone.

I wandered over to it and poured myself a cup. The coffee was lukewarm and stale. I sipped at it, wincing at the acrid taste. It was a poor substitute for Heather's coffee.

"He says he can fit you in if it's quick. He's wrapping something up, and he'll be out in a jiffy," she said, putting down the handset.

"Thanks, Peggy."

I wanted to pace the room, but I also didn't want to show too much of my nervous energy. I forced myself to take a leisurely stroll along the far wall to look through the posters instead. There were notices about how to set up neighborhood watches and various community concerns, which included things like a request for information regarding graffiti in the local park, a promise of a reward for tips on who had painted Miller Farm's Angus bull bright pink, and a reminder to register for the Island County Cook-Off before the end of the month. In the center of it all was a small section for missing persons, where a handful of pictures hung. Most of them featured runaways from across the bay in Seattle. One notice caught my attention. Peter Wright. He'd disappeared twenty-eight years ago. I was only half-surprised to see his photo still up on the wall.

He was twelve years old in the photograph. It was taken during his final year of Little League. He grinned at the camera, his blue ball cap pushed back on his head as he squinted into the sun. Blond tufts of hair stuck out around his ears. He had a smudge of dirt across his nose. He'd disappeared a few days before I was scheduled to arrive for the summer at the end of eighth grade. My trip ended up being canceled. It was the only summer I hadn't spent with my grandparents. I'd exchanged calls with Heather, Ed, and Chris about it for months, pestering them to see how the search party was going and if they'd found anything yet. The case eventually faded from the public's mind. But never the sheriff's. Peter was his son, after all.

Peggy walked up behind me. "I can't imagine coming in every day and still having to see that. Especially with everything going on."

"Did something happen?" I asked.

She nodded. "Theresa isn't doing well. Her condition's worse." Theresa was Peter's mom. Last year, she was diagnosed with cancer.

"That's terrible. Is her treatment plan not working?"

She began to say more when Bob stuck his head out of his office. "I'm ready for you."

I handed Peggy my cup and followed him in. The room was sparsely decorated, with nothing hanging on the walls. On his desk was a photo of him and Theresa. It was a few years old. She was still young and vibrant in the photo.

"What can I help you with, Miss Williams?" he asked as he took a seat. He was tall and still carried some muscle from his days playing college football. His bulky frame made his desk seem small. His salt-and-pepper hair had become more salt than pepper over the last few years.

I sat down and started fidgeting. His gaze made me feel like a child again. "Well, I'm not sure if I need to apologize or not. Leonard was in such a state over the unknown condition of Jessica's house that I offered to look at it for him. You know? Since I'm a claims adjuster, I inspect homes all the time."

"And?" He raised an eyebrow.

"Well, I just went in and didn't think about it. I hope I didn't disturb the scene or anything. If you need them, I took a bunch of photos of the place while I was there."

"The scene?"

"Yes. You know… where she died." I leaned forward in my seat and met his gaze.

He cleared his throat and sat back. "You needn't worry, Miss Williams."

"You can call me Dani," I interjected.

"All right. You needn't worry, Dani. There is no scene to disturb."

"Oh." I sank into my seat. "So they didn't find anything odd during the autopsy, then?"

He narrowed his eyes. "We don't suspect foul play."

"Isn't she a bit young?"

He nodded and cleared his throat. "It can be hard to lose a friend like this, especially so soon after your grandmother. It's natural to look for an explanation."

"Oh good, you *are* investigating—"

"I'm sure you're aware her family has a history of heart failure. It's sad, Miss Williams, but these things happen." He leaned back in his chair and spread his hands.

"She exercised. She was active."

"I know. But this isn't Seattle. This isn't Spokane. You're looking for something that just isn't there. Unless you have reason to believe she was wrapped up in something nefarious, then there isn't any reason for us to dig into her personal life."

I swallowed. *Should I show him the note? What did he mean by 'nefarious'?* Jessica had hidden the note for a reason. She'd wanted to keep it to herself. Everyone deserved their privacy. Even in death. I wavered and shook my head. I couldn't tell him about it. Not when Jessica wasn't here to defend herself.

"All right, then. Is that all?"

I nodded.

"Well, I really should start preparing for my next meeting, then. I'll see you out."

I leaped from the chair and turned toward the door. "It's okay. Thank you for your time."

I half stumbled, half ran through the lobby. Part of me expected Bob to call me back, but he didn't.

I got to my car and fumbled with my keys. *He isn't looking into her death. What's going to happen now? Is a murderer going to go free? Should I have shown him the note?* The note didn't have a date on it, so there was no way for them to know how recently she'd received it. I knew she had shoved it inside the book a week ago, but I had no way to explain how I knew. He could be right. Maybe I was searching for a boogeyman because I needed someone to blame. Someone other than me. Heart failure happens.

I dropped my keys on the ground. As I bent down to fish them out of the gravel, the door behind me opened. I glanced over my shoulder as Chris stepped out. My heart skipped a beat. I hadn't seen him in person in a long time. While Ed got to hang out with him every year at his yearly camping trip, they always met at the campsite. He looked good. He wore his brown hair cropped close to his head. His chiseled jaw was set in a frown.

Shit. He doesn't want to see me.

I surged to my feet. My hands shook as I pushed the keys into the lock. He took the stairs two at a time toward me.

"Dani," he called. He paused a few feet away, his hand raised. "Are you okay?"

I hung my head and tried to hold it together. First the divorce, then my grandmother and her lies, and now Jessica. It was too much loss for one person to handle all at once.

He crossed over to me and placed a hand on my shoulder. At that, I broke. I sobbed.

He turned me in place and pulled me in for a hug. "It's okay. Let it out. Let it out."

Why is he being so nice to me?

I breathed in his sandalwood aftershave and sank into the hug, my fingers digging into his shoulder as I cried. He was best friends with Ed. But once upon a time, he was my friend too. I'd missed him. He patted my back and consoled me while I wept.

After a minute, I pulled away. "I can't believe Jessica's gone."

"Yeah." He studied my face, concern in his eyes. "It's a shock to everyone."

"I…" I paused, wondering if he could help where the sheriff had not.

"Yes?"

"I have a bad feeling. I don't know how to describe it, but something's wrong. Not just her being dead. Something happened to her. Something bad."

"That's not an uncommon feeling. Especially when someone so young dies."

"I know," I said. "But it would ease my mind knowing how she died. Doesn't the family want to know too? Doesn't Leonard deserve answers? Shouldn't they do an autopsy so… we can all have peace of mind?"

He paused, as if choosing his next words carefully. I sensed he wanted to help me. I had always been good at reading people, but this I felt with certainty. It was an odd sensation, like a prickle at the back of my mind.

"Please," I said, tears still wet on my cheeks.

"I can see about getting one ordered. But I can't make any promises."

I nodded and reached out. "Thank you. It means a lot."

"Of course. I'll always help you out if I can."

A dark-gray Honda Odyssey pulled up. He looked over at Marsha as she got out of her car. She reached into the back seat and wrestled with a large box.

"Thank you," I said again as he stepped away from me to greet Marsha.

He nodded before turning with a smile toward her. "Hey, Marsha. Need a hand with that?"

"Oh gosh. Yes, please." She smiled back at him.

"How is the fundraising coming along?" he asked as he took the box from her.

"Fine. Although it would do better if Bob picked up his slack. I really need him on this one."

She gave me a close-lipped smile as she passed. After the door closed behind them, I got into my car and drove away.

"I'll always help you." Me specifically? *Don't be silly. Of course not. He's willing to help anyone. It's who he is. Right?* My cheeks flushed at the memory of his embrace. *What on earth did he mean by that? And why do I care?*

CHAPTER 7

Over the next few days, I barely slept. I tossed and turned every night. The dream had morphed into a recurring nightmare that chased me into my daylight hours. To keep the dreams at bay, I threw myself into work. I packed box after box and handled stack after stack of paperwork for my grandmother's estate. I searched every inch of her office for something that would explain what it meant to be a witch—something other than the journal. I reread it until I had almost memorized every page. It left me with more questions than answers. *What is the point of the Sight if I can't use it to help people?*

But whenever I paused, the threatening note and the dream would replay in my head. As I drifted off to sleep at night, I would find myself crawling across the floor of Jessica's home again and startle myself awake.

I yawned as I drove into town. I pulled to a stop at a red light and drummed my fingers against the steering wheel. *Did I make a mistake by keeping the note a secret? I wish I had heard something by now.*

My stomach growled as the light turned green. I had forgotten to restock the kitchen, and I had run out of good coffee and breakfast two days ago. At times like this, there was only one thing to do: go to the Bizzy Bean.

The dawn light crested over the water as I pulled into a spot right out front and went inside. Heather's place was known for having the best coffee in town, so despite the early hour, several patrons were already there. The center table was taken up by the Retirees, a group of women who were almost permanent fixtures at the café. They were all in their late seventies, with silver hair and brightly colored tracksuits. When they weren't here, they were going on power walks through downtown or organizing events at the community center. They had their fingers in everything in town. I nodded at them as I approached the counter.

Heather smiled at me weakly. She looked about as tired as I felt. "How are you holding up?"

"Oh, you know..." I rubbed my forehead. "Can I get a coffee and a pastry?"

"Sure thing. Your usual?"

My mouth watered at the thought of the banana-nut muffin with a salted-caramel center. "Yes. Please."

I stepped away from the counter so the person behind me could put in their order. I paused halfway across the room to watch the Retirees. Their heads bent, they whispered to each other over a box sitting between them.

"What are you ladies looking at?" I asked, making a beeline to their table.

They turned to me in unison. Sarah sat, reserved as usual, while the other two spoke. Betty and Agnes switched back and forth every other sentence. They had been together for over forty years, so finishing each other's sentences came as naturally as breathing to them.

"Oh, Dani. Just look at them! There is something precious about a mama cat nursing. I worry about the little one, though. He keeps getting edged out. Poor thing. Do you think he got anything at all?"

I peered over their shoulders into the box. It was Star and her kittens. It had been a week, and most of the kittens had almost doubled in size. But the runt of the litter was as tiny as when I'd last seen him.

"Heather?" I called out.

She came over, wiping her hands on her apron. "Yeah?"

"Has he been eating?" I lifted the little guy out of the box and held him against my chest. He nestled against my neck and tried to suck on my hair.

"Did they chase him away again? Yes. But on and off. I'll pick up some kitten formula for him when I go on break."

"Thanks. I just couldn't bear it if something happened to him too." I sniffed. The thought of losing anyone else, even a kitten, was heartbreaking. He clambered up onto my shoulder.

Heather put a hand on my arm. "It looks like you could use some kitten cuddles. Why don't we sit and chat while you eat your breakfast?"

I nodded.

I hovered over the Retirees while she went back to the counter to finish putting together my order. Sarah and Agnes quickly returned to cooing over the cats, but Betty sat staring at me. I shifted under her gaze.

"Are you feeling all right, dear?" she asked.

"I'll be fine."

"I've been meaning to drop by the agency to check in. Your gran was like an honorary member of our walking group. I was also sorry to hear about your friend. When you become an old fart like me, it's hard but not unexpected when friends pass away. But for people your age, it's got to be startling. Although, I guess you were always such a serious child with good intuition. Perhaps it wasn't as big a surprise for you."

I blinked at her. *Not a surprise? Good intuition?* I opened and closed my mouth. *How do I respond to that? Does she know I'm a witch? She couldn't. I didn't know.*

Heather popped up next to me, plate in hand. "You ready?"

I nodded, my eyes still on Betty, who smiled at me sweetly before turning back to the box.

Heather led me over to a private booth in the corner. She sat down across from me and pushed the muffin and coffee toward me. As I ate, she watched me silently. I was ravenous and took one large bite after another. The salted-caramel core melted in my mouth. I let out an appreciative sound as I savored the flavor.

"So, tell me. How are you holding up? You look tired," she said after I took my last bite.

I looked around. No one was watching us. Wordlessly, I reached into my purse and pulled out the note. I slid it to her across the table.

She read it, her eyebrows rising farther at every word. "Someone left this for you?"

I shook my head.

"Then where? Jessica's?"

I nodded.

"Oh. Oh wow." She sank into her seat.

"You're the first person I've shown it to. I thought about taking it into the station, but I was worried. What if she did something wrong, Heather?"

She straightened in her seat and held my gaze, almost as if she were daring me to disagree. "No. Jessica was a good person."

"Should I show it to them, then?" I asked.

I stroked the kitten as Heather reread the note. She frowned. "I don't know. It's an election year. I hate to say it, but Bob might rush a decision to close a case before the ballots are sent out."

"I thought he was running unopposed?"

"He is. Technically. But there's a write-in candidate that's gaining steam. It's doubtful they could close the gap. But you never know."

She pushed the note back over to me. "Did you find anything else at her house?"

"No, but to be fair, I wasn't over there looking for clues for a murder."

She nodded and looked down at her hands resting on the table. "Maybe you should."

It felt right the second she said it. I should. Someone had killed Jessica. I might find something more concrete to take to the sheriff. And if I did that, he might take the case seriously.

For the first time since finding the note, I smiled a genuine smile. *Maybe I should.*

"Thanks, Heather." I picked up my stuff and headed for the door.

She laughed. "Aren't you forgetting something?"

I turned to her, confused.

She chuckled again. "The kitten."

"Oh. Right!" I reached into my hair. He had made himself a small nest at the crook of my neck. I pulled him out and placed him gently back down in the box with his brothers and sisters.

"You'll buy him the kitten formula?" I asked.

"Of course. Now, go find yourself a clue."

I grinned. "I plan on it."

CHAPTER 8

I climbed into my car and sat there, my hands hovering over the wheel. The biohazard cleanup company could show up any day now, if they hadn't already been there. If they disturbed the scene, I could miss something important. I had to go now. I pulled out my phone and dialed Olivia. She picked up on the second ring.

"Hey, Liv. I know we had plans to go over the client list this morning, but I was wondering if we could do it after lunch instead? There are a few things I have to take care of first." I bit my lip.

"I should be able to," she said, panting into the phone. "I'm taking my walk right now. But I'll be around all day, assuming the little guy remains stubborn. I'll have Zach message you if I end up going into labor." Zach, her husband, was an elementary school teacher. He was off for the summer and waiting in the wings in case he was needed.

"It's been such a hectic week, I almost forgot we were past your due date. What are you doing in the office?"

"It's either this or be at home and live through Debby hovering. She really needs to be focusing on Dad's campaign instead of refluffing my foot pillows for the seventh time in an hour," she said.

I barked out a laugh. Deborah Bishop was a true mother hen. She not only owned the grocery store but also ran the local food pantry. It was like her personal mission that no one would go hungry on her watch. "At this rate, you really are going to give birth in the office. Debby would have a field day over that. Are you sure you want to risk her wrath?"

"I've got Zach on speed dial. The second I feel a contraction, I'll call him. Don't worry. I'll see you after lunch."

I chuckled again before hanging up and drove straight to Jessica's house.

I parked across the street. The sky was clear, and the sun hung low on the horizon, bathing her home in a warm glow. Light sparkled off the windows and the water in the stone birdbath in her front yard. It really was a beautiful property. I stared up at it for a minute before getting out of the car.

I picked up the key from under the frog and let myself in, setting my home-inspection kit next to the door. It was strange. I hadn't been inside the house in a few days, but I had an excellent memory. Someone had come through and moved almost every item in the room. A few inches here, a few inches there. A vase of flowers that had been sitting near the edge of the end table was now centered. I inhaled deeply. It was faint, but the unmistakable scent of cleaner lingered in the air.

I slumped forward, hanging my head. The cleaners had already come through.

What're the chances I'll find anything now? I shook my head and straightened my shoulders. *Zero, if I don't look.*

I prowled through the living room, opening every drawer and cabinet door. I riffled through the papers and looked behind all the decorations. The papers were mostly owner's manuals or fliers for craft fairs. I peeked inside the last container in the entertainment center and found a DVD collection. Most of the movies were at least ten years old, and a thin layer of dust coated the top. I slid the box onto the shelf and stepped away from the cabinet. I turned, looking around the room again. *What now?*

I smiled as the thought came to me. *Check where the cleaning crew wouldn't have gone.* I strode through the house to the back door and went outside to look around Jessica's workshop.

Her workshop, which was inside a remodeled red barn, was almost as big as the house. I lifted the roll-up doors. To the left were her van and commuter car, and on the right was a sprawling woodworking station. A half-finished wooden boat hung from the rafters.

I started with the vehicles. Jessica had left them unlocked. The car was a black Hyundai Accent. Attached to the back seat was a small trash can filled with empty water bottles. The central console held a bottle of Advil, a pair of sunglasses, and sunblock. There wasn't anything other than her registration and title in the glove compartment. The trunk only had a spare tire and a jack.

I bit my lip and moved on to the older model Ford Transit Van with a faded sign on the side that read Johnson's Custom Carpentry. The front seat was as exciting as the car. I got out to check the back. When I opened the doors, my breath caught in my throat. The cat tower sat in the center of the van, taking up almost every spare inch. I sniffled and wiped a tear from my face. The cat tower was the last thing we had spoken about, and here it was. Five stories tall, with ramps going between four towers, it was as beautiful as Jessica claimed. There were countless hidey-holes and posts covered in scratchable material.

I climbed into the back and looked through the tower. Nothing. There were no notes or clues tucked away. Dejected, I climbed back out of the van and plodded over to the woodworking station.

Pieces of wood, resin mixing bowls, splatters of paint, and a glass sculpture of an orchid covered the workbenches. I searched through all of it but found nothing there either. I retraced my steps through the barn, ending at the workbench a second time.

"Okay," I whispered to myself. "If I were a clue, where would I be?" She had so few personal items out here. There were no photos, only a set of speakers and a coffee cup. *A coffee cup?* I replayed the dream in my head. *Ceramic. In the dream, I crawled over broken ceramic.*

I opened my eyes and strode back to the house to grab a flashlight from my kit. I started by the chair, shining my flashlight in every nook and cranny, searching for a single piece that had been missed. As I prowled past the heat vent on the floor, the light caught the edge of something white at the bottom. I crouched next to the vent and shone my flashlight between the slats. Sitting at the bottom of the air duct was a single shard of ceramic. I grinned and put the flashlight between my teeth to lever the heat register up and reach into it.

I lay on the floor, my arm shoved all the way into the register. The vent pipe was deeper than I had originally thought. My fingers slid across the bottom, groping for the sliver of ceramic in the dark. I caught the edge of it with my nails and slid it closer. A sense of frustration and urgency, mixed with a need to have the shard and anger it was out of reach, filled me. It had that same foreign feeling the condolence cards and journal had. It wasn't something *I* felt—it was a memory of someone else's emotion. I wrapped my hand around the shard gingerly and pulled it out.

I sat on the floor, my legs splayed out in front of me, and turned it over in my hand, scrutinizing it from every angle. The shard was about an inch long and half an inch wide. *Now what?*

I bit my lip and studied the shard. It was slightly curved

and white, with a pink rose on one side. The edges were sharp where it had broken off. The piece looked like it was from my dream, but I couldn't be sure.

I took a shaky breath and closed my eyes. *All right, Grandma. If I'm a witch and I have the Sight, show me something.* I held the shard in my palm and cleared my mind.

"Show me something important," I whispered.

Nothing happened.

I opened one eye and peeked down at the shard. It looked the same. I retrieved my bag and sat back down on the floor. My hands shaking, I rummaged through it for my grandmother's journal. My fingers closed around the leather cover. I pulled it out and searched for a specific page. I stopped when I found it.

My grandmother had written a few different variations of a memory spell. It ranged in complexity from relatively simple to a sixteen-step hour-long ritual. It was a purposeful activation of the Sight. While I inherently knew the most recent or strongest emotion someone felt as they interacted with an object when I touched it, I never knew the context. This spell would allow me to experience an event from the object's perspective.

Why did I see Jessica's body before she died? The thought popped into my head out of nowhere. I couldn't help it, but when I closed my eyes, I could still picture her lying there, her face covered by her hair and her arm outstretched toward me. I flipped from page to page, searching for the answer. My hands trembled. *Stop it. Focus on the task at hand. I can figure that part out later.*

I turned back to the memory spell. The simplest version would let me experience flashes of important moments from an object's recent history. The more complex the spell, the further back I could delve. I wasn't confident enough in my abilities to do a complex version yet. And I didn't need it in this situation. What I needed was basic. *What happened to this cup?*

I kneeled on the floor with my grandmother's journal on one side and the shard on the other. My grandmother's words lingered in my mind. *Intention is everything.* I scanned through the directions a few more times until the spell and my intention were solid in my head. I exhaled and shook out my arms.

I whispered the words of the spell again. Motes of light danced in the air where my breath had been. They cascaded through the air and settled onto my hand, causing it to glow a soft white light. "Wow." I gaped at my hand. *Is this what magic looks like?* I shook my head and refocused. *Show me something important.*

I touched the shard, and a cool sensation coursed through me as the white light flowed from my fingertips and into the shard. The light pulsed and shimmered. It swirled around my hand and the shard, covering both in a golden haze.

I could still distantly feel the floor beneath me and the shard under my fingers, but for the rest of my body, it was almost as if I were the shard. I sank back against the ground as the cool sensation spread through me.

Oh my gosh. I'm doing it. I'm casting a spell. Cool wind blew over me. Something large, almost the size of my torso, and soft brushed against my skin. *Are those fingertips?* I tried to focus on the sensation. *Are those my fingertips or the killer's?* They brushed against me once, twice, three times. That was longer than it had taken me to grab onto the piece.

Above me, a floorboard creaked.

I gasped, sitting up. The squeak wasn't from the vision. It was here and now. I scrambled to my feet, thrusting the journal back into my bag. As I inched toward the hallway, I shoved the shard into my pocket. Clenching my teeth, I took a faltering step forward. I paused at the archway to the hall as another floorboard creaked overhead. I fished my phone out of my pocket and dialed 911. My finger hovered over the call button. *What if it's Leonard? It's technically his house now.*

I took another hesitant step toward the hallway and peered around the corner as a woman came down the stairs. Her shoulder-length black hair was up in a high ponytail. It shone under the light. She was breathtakingly beautiful, her face and figure perfectly sculpted. I scurried backward. She froze, and her head whipped in my direction. I ducked out of sight behind the wall.

Footsteps pounded down the last few stairs and onto the tile of the kitchen. They began to retreat away from me, toward the back door. *Oh, no, you don't.* I dropped my phone and dove for my kit at the door. I grabbed the camera and dashed after her. The rear door slammed shut behind her. I sprinted toward the door, ripping off the lens cover as I moved. My foot caught on an area rug rolled up next to the wall, and I slid to my knees.

I scrambled to my feet and threw open the back door. Pain shot through my legs as I limped through the door. I lifted my camera and snapped a single shot of her as she vaulted over the fence in one smooth motion. I stumbled across the yard, trying to capture another picture, but she was gone.

My heart raced. My hands fumbled as I checked the camera. The shot was blurry, and she was out of focus. I sighed and dropped my hands to my sides.

I backtracked to the kitchen and retrieved my phone and lens cover from the floor. I cursed under my breath as the screen came to life and I found a new crack in the corner. It was still prepped to dial the police. I jumped as my phone rang in my hand.

It was Chris.

"I have an update for you," he said, his voice tired.

"Oh?" My mind flashed to the woman. *Did he see her somehow? Does he know where I am?*

"Preliminary findings have come back. Jessica died from hemlock poisoning."

My heart skipped a beat. I held out my hand to steady myself against the wall. "Poisoned? Someone killed her?" I had known it already, but hearing someone else say it made it different somehow. More real. It wasn't a dream or a strange vision. My friend had been murdered.

"I wanted you to hear it from me first." He paused for a few seconds before continuing. "I have to bring Heather in for questioning."

"Heather?" I gasped.

"Yes," he sighed.

"But it can't be Heather, Chris. I'm at Jessica's house right now, and I just saw someone break in. It definitely wasn't Heather."

"Are you okay?"

"Yeah. I'm fine. But don't you see? It can't be Heather! I just chased someone out the back door, and it wasn't her." I gripped the phone.

"It's going to be okay. Breathe. Did you recognize them?"

"No, but… I got a good look at them. I would recognize her if I saw her again."

"Come in and give a statement when you can. But, Dani, I have to follow orders. I'm bringing Heather in. It's only for questioning. We found a tea bag filled with hemlock in the trash inside a Bizzy Bean cup. If she didn't do it, I'm sure she will be fine. I've got to go. Stay safe, okay?"

"I will."

He hung up, and I gaped at my phone. *Heather? How could anyone think Heather would do something like this?*

I dialed her number. It rang a few times before going to voicemail. I dialed her again. "Pick up. Pick up. Pick up." Her voicemail answered again. I stared wide-eyed at my phone. *I have to warn her.*

I dashed for my car.

CHAPTER 9

During the hour I'd been at Jessica's, the roadways had become congested with traffic. I shook in my seat, impatient to get to the Bizzy Bean. I dialed Heather again. It went to voicemail once more. I slammed my palm on the steering wheel. I had this sinking feeling they had already taken her in and I had missed my opportunity. The suspicion was confirmed as I pulled up in front of the café. All the patrons were standing out on the sidewalk, watching as Chris put Heather into the back seat of the patrol car.

I slowed and inched down the roadway, searching for an empty parking space. Every spot was filled. Chris closed the door behind Heather. I swerved and parked at the side of the road. A car honked behind me. The driver glared at me as they edged around my vehicle. I jumped out of my car and dashed toward Chris, pushing my way through the swarm of people milling about the sidewalk.

"Wait!" I yelled, but the crowd drowned out my voice. *He can't hear me.* I slipped past a group of teenagers, sidestepped Marsha, and surged forward, my hand raised, as Chris shut his door.

"Wait!" I yelled again, tears of frustration in my eyes. He

drove away without once looking in my direction. *He didn't see me.*

The group on the curb murmured to each other and broke apart. I hung my head and balled my hands into fists, my whole body shaking. "Dang it."

Betty stepped forward and put a hand on my shoulder. "It's going to be okay, dear."

"They've got the wrong person," I cried.

The Retirees nodded in unison. "I know. Heather would never hurt anyone."

I wiped my eyes. "I came here from Jessica's."

The last large group of customers dispersed down the street, leaving me alone with the Retirees. They surrounded me and began asking questions. It was hard to make out what any of them said as they spoke over each other. Betty batted Agnes and Sarah away and turned me around to face her.

"Don't mind them," she said, squeezing my shoulders. "It looks like you have something you need to get off your chest. What is it?"

I nodded, still dazed by the experience. "I was just at Jessica's, and there was someone in her house. It was a woman. She must have broken in. When she saw me, she ran."

They all gasped, once again in unison.

"She had dark hair. Athletic build. About this tall." I held my hand up a few inches over my head. "She was... beautiful."

Betty looked over at Agnes and Sarah. They nodded, stepped aside, and huddled together to confer. After almost a minute, Agnes turned toward me. She pulled out her phone and held it out. She had the local community theater website up, and on the front page was the woman.

"That's her!" I gasped.

They exchanged a glance, and Agnes handed me her

phone. "Her name is Vanessa Bennett. She lives in the same neighborhood as Jess."

"They're members of the same HOA. Jessica's the chairperson," Betty continued.

Sarah picked up where Betty left off. "And Vanessa was constantly skirting the HOA rules. Last year, she tried to paint her house purple. Purple, can you believe it?"

"Jessica had to send her the letter telling her she had to repaint or face fines from the association," Agnes continued. "Vanessa was not pleased. Ever since, they've had this back-and-forth spat."

"It was almost like a modern-day feud," Sarah finished.

I studied her face. "It was definitely her."

"Do you think she had something to do with Jessica's death?" Agnes asked.

"She might have. I don't know." I handed Agnes her phone back.

"She's online all the time," Sarah said. "She's a bit of a local celebrity."

Betty rolled her eyes. "A retired model. She does community theater these days. I wouldn't call that a celebrity."

"She's in the Arts and Entertainment section of the *Island County Gazette* all the time. I think that counts," Agnes piped in. At that, they bickered.

If she and Jessica were feuding, Vanessa might be the killer. I racked my brain, trying to figure out why she could have been at the house. A sign. A clue. A piece of evidence tying her to the scene. *Was it the ceramic shard? Should I try to cast the spell on the shard again?*

I sighed. The brief flash I'd received earlier wasn't helpful. *I need to figure out how to use these powers. Should I try the more complicated ritual?* My palms became sweaty, and I swallowed. *Let's try some good old-fashioned investigative work first. I'll try magic later if this doesn't work.*

As the Retirees talked, I pulled out my phone and searched for Vanessa on social media. I found her profile easily enough and scrolled through her various posts. Sarah was right— Vanessa was online a lot. She posted several times a day. She had a lot of selfies with carefully placed local area merchandise in the background. While she may have retired from the runway, she seemed to be growing her brand as a local area influencer. The past week, however, was barren compared to her usual amount of activity. Under a selfie outside a hotel from a week ago was a caption saying that she was going to be offline for a few days for some much-needed R & R. There were no other posts until this morning, when she posted a photo of her morning coffee with *#firstcupfriday* underneath.

"It looks like she may have been out of town all week," I said.

The ladies stopped bickering to peer over my shoulder at my phone.

"It says she was away, but she could always have come back," Sarah said.

"True." I opened the photo of her standing in front of the hotel. She had a secretive smile, with sunglasses perched on top of her head. I read through the caption again. It said she was staying at Reginald's, but there was no location data. I couldn't find any obvious landmarks in the photo. I did a quick search for the name and couldn't find a place locally. Reginald's could have been anywhere.

"Can you look up other people on that thing?" Betty asked.

"Yes," I said, closing the photo. "Why?"

"Well, do you have any other suspects? Couldn't you look them up too?" she asked.

I blinked. *Richard? Leonard?* Digging into these things was exciting. I wasn't sure how it happened, but I had stumbled into the role of investigator. I couldn't bear the idea of

Heather being arrested for a crime she didn't commit. "Richard."

"Yeah. He's probably a good place to start. I heard somewhere that it's common for partners to have done it," Betty said.

"Those are with crimes of passion," Agnes cut in.

I nodded. "I saw them arguing the morning before."

Betty glared at Agnes. "See? It's worth looking into."

Agnes waved Betty off. "Leonard, maybe? He was her only family left. That was close, anyway."

"How about Thomas?" Sarah asked.

Agnes cocked her head to one side. "Why Thomas?"

"Because he's an exterminator. I'm sure he knows better than most people how to handle poisonous stuff." Sarah puffed up her chest.

"If you add him, then you would have to add most of the local farmers. You might as well add my brother to that list, if that's your criteria. You can't forget about a motive in your name-calling." Agnes put her hands on her hips, and the bickering continued. It was a lighthearted affair. They had been friends since they were children.

Richard was a good candidate. It would be a little unusual for a man to use poison, but it isn't unheard of. He had the access. Leo also had access. They weren't as close as they used to be, but he still loved her. At least, I thought he did. *I wish I had Heather here to bounce ideas off of.*

I typed the names into my phone. Richard and Leonard didn't go online much. Most of their social media, or at least public profiles, were about work functions. Richard was an architect. He shared a lot of articles about construction and new trends in the business. Leonard worked for a big tech firm in Seattle, and his profile was very similar. Thomas wasn't online, but like Sarah had said, he had no reason to hurt Jessica. They didn't exactly run in the same circles. After a few minutes of searching, the only good lead I could find was Vanessa.

"Thanks, ladies," I said. "You've been very helpful."

They beamed and said they would think about it more. I watched them walk away down the street. Without their favorite coffee shop, they would move on to the local area mall for their walk. I smiled, imagining their lazy days, and turned to my car, which was still double-parked. Cars were inching carefully around it. Oncoming traffic honked as I dashed toward it.

I have to take this to Chris. If they know about Vanessa, maybe they'll stop investigating the wrong person. I slid in behind the wheel. I sent a quick text to Olivia to let her know I was going to be a little later than expected and headed straight to the sheriff's office.

CHAPTER 10

The gravel crunched under my tires as I pulled into the sheriff station parking lot. It was a small lot, and I slid into one of the few remaining open spots. I surged out of my car and strode toward the front door. I faltered halfway. In the short row of cars, I recognized most of them from my last visit. A new-model red Audi S5 stood out. The car was polished and gleamed under the midday sun. Parked between the older-model Dodge Chargers and dust-covered Ford pickups, it stood out like a sore thumb.

I slowed my pace as I approached the vehicle. The plates were local and still had the Audi Bellevue license plate frame. I glanced at the sheriff's office. Peggy sat behind the reception desk, her eyes on me. I pulled out my phone and stopped next to the car. While I angled my head toward my phone, I peered out of the corner of my eye inside the car. It was clean, almost like a newly acquired rental. As my eyes flicked back to the main door, a sticker on the windshield caught my attention. It was a parking sticker for an architecture firm in Seattle. *An architect? Isn't Richard an architect? What are the chances there's another one here?*

My eyes flicked back and forth from the vehicle to Peggy

behind the front desk. Her gaze was focused straight on me, her brow furrowed. *Shoot. I've got to keep moving. There's no time for a spell. And she might see it. Shimmering lights aren't exactly discreet.*

As I continued to walk to the trailer, my hand darted out, and I ran my fingers over the car door. At first, it didn't seem like it worked. The tightness in my chest swelled. I swallowed, pushing the lump in my throat down. *Anxiety? What does that mean?* I straightened and marched up the porch steps.

Peggy gave me a tight-lipped smile and cleared her throat as I walked into the foyer. "Hey, Dani. Is there something I can help you with?"

"Is Chris available? I need to talk to him."

"He's not right now, unfortunately. What do you need to talk to him about? Maybe there is someone else who can help you." She reached for the phone, her hand hovering over the receiver.

"He suggested I come in." I shoved my hands into my pockets, fighting the urge to fidget with the strap of my purse.

Her smile wavered, and she opened and closed her mouth a few times before finding the words. "Oh, gosh. I see. Does this have something to do with Heather?"

"Not exactly. I have information that might be important, though. I can wait if he'll be a while."

She exhaled, blowing her cheeks out as she shook her head. "I think it might be best if you spoke with Sheriff Wright. He's heading up the investigation. Hold on a second, and I'll give him a ring."

"Okay." I sighed and took a step back from her desk.

She picked up the handset and turned away from me in her seat. She lowered her voice and half covered the mouthpiece with her hand. I cocked my head to one side and studied her. After a short exchange, she turned back to me, a hesitant smile on her face. "He's going to be a few minutes and asked if you could wait in the interview room."

"The interview room?"

She coughed and rubbed at the back of her neck. "Yeah. It's down the hall. He's in a meeting right now. I'll take you there."

I followed Peggy down the hall. The manufactured home had three bedrooms; the master bedroom had been repurposed into the sheriff's office and the two smaller bedrooms into interview rooms. I glanced into the first room as I walked past. Heather sat hunched over a small wooden table with a cup of coffee clasped between her hands. Her normally pale skin was ashen. Her eyes were wide and unblinking as she shook her head.

Peggy whisked me down the hall and into an almost-identical room next door. The blinds were drawn over the window AC unit, leaving the room cold but dim. Peggy wavered in the doorway, wringing her hands. "He might be a few minutes. Did you need anything to drink while you wait, dear?"

"No thanks."

Peggy jerked her head down and darted back out into the hall. Her shuffling footsteps faded down the hall. I lingered near the shared wall with Heather. The steady hum of the AC drowned out the muffled voices. I paced the room as the minutes ticked by.

At first, I counted my passes, but after I passed one hundred turns, I lost track of how many times my feet carried me across the room. I stopped in the middle of the room and rolled my shoulders. My joints popped. I squinted at the door. Peggy had left it open an inch. I edged toward it and peered out into the hallway. At the end of the hall, Peggy sat behind her desk. Her fingers flew across her keyboard in a flurry of movement. Her glasses sat perched on the tip of her nose.

The door to the sheriff's office opened. I darted back, away from the door. *What am I doing?* I shook my head and stepped back up to the doorway. Richard stepped out into the hallway. He wore black slacks and a dark-blue button-up shirt with the top button of his collar undone. He shuffled forward, his shoulders slumped. Bob stepped into the hall after him. They spoke to each other in hushed tones, shook hands, and parted ways.

I scurried away from the door and sat down on the plastic chair. It creaked under me as my leg bounced.

"Miss Williams." Sheriff Wright closed the door behind him.

"Hi, Bob." I twisted in my seat toward him. He glowered at me. I swallowed and stilled my leg. "I mean, Sheriff Wright."

He didn't move from the doorway. Instead, he stood there, looming over me. My eyes flicked between him, the window, and the sparse furnishings. I recognized his tactics. This was all window dressing. People talked more when they were uncomfortable. Now that I recognized it for what it was, the tension in my shoulders eased. I relaxed into the chair.

"I heard you have information. I must admit, I was surprised since the last time you came in, you said you didn't have anything. Is there a reason you're coming forward now?" he asked, breaking the silence.

"I have new information. And well, last time I was here, you told me you didn't suspect foul play. I didn't realize I knew anything important." I turned away from him and leaned back in my chair.

"New information?" He joined me at the table. He sat across from me, frowning.

"Yes. This might be better with Chris. I've already half told him about it already."

"He isn't available. So why don't you save both of us time

and tell me." He pulled out a notepad and opened it to an empty page.

"I just came from Jessica's house."

"And?" His pen hovered over the page.

"I saw a woman at her home." I studied him as I spoke. His eyes flicked up to me and back down at the page. "Her name is Vanessa Bennet. She broke in—"

"Did you see signs of forced entry?" he asked, cutting me off.

"No, but—"

"Go on." He cut in again.

"She was in the house." I shifted in my seat. While I recognized the tactics, it was still off-putting.

"And how did you get in?"

"Leo told me where to find the spare key. I've been helping him with a few things."

"And then what happened?" he asked.

"I saw her in the house. She seemed to be looking for something. When she saw me, she bolted out the back door. From what I've heard, she was in some sort of feud with Jessica over HOA business. Have you checked her out yet?"

"We are exploring all avenues of investigation. In fact, we have a suspect in for questioning right now." He grinned.

Is he gloating? My pulse pounded in my ears. *Is he happy about bringing in Heather?* I leaned forward in my chair, and my words tumbled out of my mouth before I could stop them. "Heather? Because of a tea bag in the trash? That seems like a stretch. I mean, what about the broken coffee cup?"

His head jerked up. "Where did you hear that?" he asked through gritted teeth.

I blinked. "I was there. I saw it."

"For a home inspection?"

"Yes?"

"Do home inspections usually involve going through someone's trash?"

"No…" *What does this have to do with a broken cup?*

"Then why were you?" He leaned toward me until he was perched at the edge of his seat.

"I didn't." I stammered.

"Then how"—he spat his words—"did you know about the tea bag?"

Was that supposed to be a secret? Why did Chris tell me? I shifted in my seat and made a show of thinking. *If I tell him the truth, will Chris get in trouble? Lie.* "I heard it somewhere. I think it was one of the Retirees. I just came from the Bizzy Bean. They were all standing out front."

"I thought you said you came here from Jessica's."

"I did. I was at Jessica's, and I stopped by the Bizzy Bean on my way here."

"I see." He relaxed into his chair.

"But what about the broken coffee cup?"

"What broken coffee cup?" He blinked.

"The one in the living room. I saw it there, on the floor."

"There was no broken coffee cup in the living room."

I grabbed my bag from the table and fished out my camera. I scrolled through the photos until I reached the set of the living room. I stared at the screen. There was no broken cup in any of them. *It was there. I saw it.* I dropped the camera to my lap. *I saw it in my dream.*

"Well, let's see it." He held out his hand.

I blinked and handed it to him. "At least, I assumed there was one. There was a puddle of tea. It didn't show up well in the photos. I'm sorry."

"Do you have any other photos of the scene?"

"Yes, most of them are still on there," I said.

"Did you download any of them?"

"I have a few on my laptop." I gestured weakly to my bag. *It was gone before I got there. Someone cleaned it before I showed up. Heather? No. She wouldn't hurt a fly. And even if she were capable of it, why would she leave the tea bag?*

"I'm going to need your camera and your laptop," he said, interrupting my train of thought.

"Excuse me?" I gaped at him.

"They may have evidence on them. I'm going to take them into evidence."

"But you can't…" I stammered.

"Miss Williams, we will return your property back once we've cleared them."

"I can send you the photos."

"Do you realize that interfering in a police investigation is a crime?"

I blinked. "I do."

"Well, then, you will get them back once we've cleared them." He frowned at me. "Is there any other relevant information you might have?"

I sat there, blinking. My mind whirled through the possibilities. *Heather knows about the note and might have already mentioned it. This could be a test. Or... it could be a fishing expedition.* I studied him over the table.

"Are you going to look into Vanessa?" I asked, stalling for time.

"We are looking at multiple avenues of investigation."

"What about Richard? I mean, they were close. And I saw them arguing the morning before she died."

"We considered him a person of interest, but he has an alibi. Now, please answer the question. Do you have any other relevant information?" He set the camera down.

His jaw was clenched, but the rest of his face was impassive. He was holding himself in check so I couldn't read his body language. My eyes flicked to the camera and back to him. I learned forward and rested my hand on the table. My fingers inched forward until I touched the strap.

Contempt.

The only emotion I got back when I touched the strap was disdain. I blinked. *He isn't taking me seriously. He's not going to look into anything I give him.* Holding his gaze, I let the feeling settle into me and smiled. I pulled out my laptop and handed it to him. "I wish I knew more that could help you."

He stood and held the door open for me. "A deputy will call you when you can come pick up your belongings."

I nodded and strode out into the hallway. His eyes burrowed into my back as I retreated down the hall. Heather still sat in her interrogation room. She was alone, tears streaking down her face. She hugged herself, shivering as the AC blew directly onto her.

They're not going to take anything I tell them seriously. If they won't investigate the real leads, then I will. I stalked out to my car. *Three suspects. One good lead. Let's start by busting Vanessa's alibi.*

CHAPTER 11

I drove straight to the agency. Without my laptop, finding the hotel Vanessa had stayed at was going to be difficult. I needed access to a computer, and my grandmother had one at her desk. When I arrived at the office, I found Olivia camped out in the break room. She had wedged her rolling chair into a corner and stacked a pile of boxes in front of it. She sat with her back against the wall, with her feet up on a suit jacket folded into a makeshift pillow. Her shoes had been kicked off next to her on the floor. Her ankles were swollen and puffy.

"Don't you dare tell Debbie," she said when I stepped into the room.

The stress from the day bubbled out of me. I laughed. For a few seconds, thoughts of Jessica's murder disappeared. Olivia looked miserable, and all she cared about was avoiding her mother. In comparison, it was a minor issue. But it reminded me that life around me continued, and someday soon, hopefully, my worries would be small again too.

"I won't. I promise. Scout's honor." I wiped a tear from

my face. *Shoot. The client list. She's been waiting.* "Are you still good to go through the client list with me?"

She leaned her head back and groaned. "I don't know. I've organized it, but honestly, I need to start moving before the swelling overtakes the rest of my body."

"Where are they? I can read through them and call you if I have questions," I said.

She nodded. "That sounds lovely. Help me up."

I grinned, stepped forward, and held out my arm for her to grab. She grasped onto my forearms and levered herself up. She waddled to her desk and returned to a few file folders. I flipped through them as she gave me a quick rundown of what type of policy was in each folder: auto, homeowners, farm, and so on. She had color-coordinated the clients who had multiple policies. "I'll be back in ten minutes." She exhaled sharply and placed her hand over her stomach. "Or not. He's kicking up a storm. I'll text you, okay?" she said over her shoulder as she slipped on her shoes. She switched the sign on the door to Closed and hobbled out.

I didn't have the heart to tell her about Heather. After the door swung shut, I slumped into my chair. The image of Heather shivering and alone in the interview room lingered in my mind. I sighed and sat up. *Don't wallow. Wallowing will help no one. But Heather...* I shook my head and reached for the keyboard. As my fingers came into contact with the keys, my heartbeat quickened.

The last time I had used the computer, I had only been half-focused on the work as flashes of the dream played through my mind. My emotions still remained on the keys. I shook my hands and exhaled slowly through my mouth. Once the sensation was gone, I reached out. Once again, the second I touched the keyboard, the emotions came back. But this time, they were stronger. This time, the fear over Heather was mixed in.

I forced myself to continue typing. With each keystroke,

it became worse. My insides quivered as I opened Vanessa's profile. My heart hammered as I copied the photo of her outside of the hotel and dropped it into Google's image search. I blinked, trying to focus on the task at hand. As I clicked Search, my breathing became so fast, I could barely suck in enough air before gasping for another breath.

I stood and stumbled back from the keyboard. *What's happening to me?* I staggered away from the desk. Each item I touched flooded my body with different responses. I hugged my arms to my body as I lurched toward the bathroom. I slammed the door shut behind me and turned on the water. The sudden coolness of it snapped me back to the present. I splashed my face again and let the water run over my hands until my heartbeat had settled. *What was that? Relax. Breathe.*

I closed my eyes and counted backward from ten, breathing slowly through my nose. My eyes flew open, and my head jerked toward the bathroom door as the front door chimed on *one*.

"I'm back!" Olivia shouted. "I know. I didn't make it far, but my phone kept buzzing."

Olivia shuffled around the office on the other side of the door. Her voice was muffled through the wood. I only caught every other word. She was discussing a claim with a desk adjuster on the phone. I splashed my face one last time and tentatively touched the door. There was a moment of emotion, which quickly faded. I steadied my breathing and opened the door.

"Yeah. It's a pity about Erickson," Olivia said, a little louder. "It really is too bad there aren't any good independent adjusters in the area. I'll let you know if I hear about any new ones setting up shop."

I half smiled as I shuffled back to the desk. She was not so subtly hinting I should stay in the area and open up my own firm after I dealt with Gran's estate. *There is no way I could stay, though, right?* I'd told my daughter I would only be here through the summer. She would be home from her camping trip in a few weeks and would need me there. *Won't she?* I clenched my jaw. *No. No, she won't.* She would be at university in the fall. She wouldn't need me there. Maybe I should stay. Once she was off to school, there would be nothing in Spokane for me to go back to. No job. No marriage. No family.

I stood over the desk, my hand hovering over the keyboard. *Is it safe? Has whatever that was passed?* I bit my lip and put my hand down. There was a flash of emotion, which faded as I moved my fingers to another key.

I breathed a sigh of relief and sat down. The image-search results were on the screen. I scrolled through them. The problem with Vanessa being a model was so many of the photos were of her. About halfway down the page was the first match that didn't include her face. It was of a building in downtown Seattle. I pulled it up and zoomed in, my eyes flicking from Vanessa's photo to the result. It was a match.

"What are you looking at there?" Olivia asked.

I jumped as she sat down at the edge of the desk.

"You startled me," I said, giggling nervously.

She laughed. "I noticed. Hopefully, it's at least something fun that's got you so distracted."

"It's nothing. A bit of research."

She peered at my screen. "Is that Reginald's?"

I bolted upright. "You know Reginald's?"

"I stayed there for my anniversary last year. It's a bit out of my normal price range, but I wanted it to be special. And because of my dad's connections, we were able to get a room."

"Oh, where is it? It looks like it's in Seattle, but I can't find a listing for it online."

"You wouldn't. It's actually called Pacific Garden, but the owner likes to give everything a personal touch. His motto is while you're there, you're family. He's Reginald."

"Thank you." Seattle was a short ferry ride away. I finally had a place to start. I tried to smile.

"Are you okay?" she asked.

"It's been a rough day."

Olivia put her hand on my shoulder. "You want to talk about it?"

"I don't know. Maybe? I stopped by Jessica's to help Leo with some stuff... and someone had broken into her house. And then I found out the sheriff brought Heather in for questioning."

"Questioning? For what?"

"Jessica's murder," I cried.

Her jaw dropped. She blinked and shook her head. "Murder? Heather? Are you sure?"

"I saw her driven away in the sheriff's car. They had her in the back seat. But it wasn't her who broke into Jessica's. It was this woman here. " I zoomed out on the photo of Vanessa so Olivia could see it. "I went by the station to give them my statement. I don't know if it helped at all."

"Wow." She shook her head again. "No wonder you're out of it. First, your grandmother, and now this. You've only been in town for a few days, and already, the few friends you have are... Well, how are you holding up? Are you going to be okay?"

I rubbed at the bridge of my nose. "Honestly? I don't know. I know they are looking at the wrong person. Heather wouldn't hurt a fly."

"Everyone knows that."

"Not the sheriff, apparently." I shrugged.

"You should go rest. Take your mind off things for a while."

"I've got to review these lists." I gestured.

She looked down at the stack of papers. "It can wait until next week. You really look like you could use some time to decompress."

She was right. I would not be of any use in my current state. "All right. Thanks, Liv. I'll see you on Monday?"

"Of course. Well, assuming this little guy is still being stubborn." She patted her belly. "Text me if you need anything. I'm serious, Dani. Anything. You're not alone in this."

I nodded, stood, and gathered my things. I might not be alone in this, but right then, I was sure Heather felt like she was, and I had to remedy that situation. While I needed to decompress, the idea of sitting around the house, waiting to hear an update, made my stomach convulse. I needed to be out there. If Sheriff Wright insisted on looking into Heather, I would look into someone a lot more likely.

Vanessa.

CHAPTER 12

I went straight from the office to the docks and took the ferry into Seattle. The entire ride, I sat hunched over my phone, scrolling through the various profiles of the potential suspects. Vanessa still seemed like the best bet, but I couldn't rule out Richard or Leonard. The morning Jessica died, Richard had fought with her outside the bank. And while Leonard seemed distraught about her death, he was rushing through things quickly.

Are the tears guilt instead of grief? I scrolled through Leonard's feed one last time before the boat pulled up to the dock. I shoved my phone into my pocket and joined the mass of people descending the stairs to their cars from the observation deck above. Leonard was at the bottom of my list, but I wasn't ready to take him off it yet.

Once off the ferry, I followed my GPS to the Denny Triangle. Glass skyscrapers towered over the street. Between them sat stone buildings that had been there since the turn of the twentieth century. Old and new structures crowded each other for space. While the ferry ride had been relatively short, in my infinite wisdom, I had come to Seattle at the end of the business day on a Friday. Traffic moved through the streets at a slow crawl. It took me over twenty minutes to circle the block, looking for a spot to park. The roads were steep, with every inch of parking space filled with cars jammed together. On my second loop, I finally caved and pulled into a garage. I almost turned back around when I read the price, but if I could prove Vanessa wasn't out of town like she claimed, it would be worth it.

When I stepped out onto the sidewalk, I looked around for the Pacific Garden. There wasn't a sign for the hotel anywhere. I checked the map on my phone again. According to my GPS, I was standing outside it. I glanced up and down the street and double-checked my phone. I paced the sidewalk, searching for the sign. A large brick building took up the entire block; a metal placard for Atlas Apartments hung over the entrance. As I walked past for the third time, I noticed a second doorway halfway down the building. It was a plain wooden door with a number next to it. I rechecked the address. This was the place. I stared at it. *How could this be a hotel?*

I shook my head as I tried the handle. The door swung open, revealing a lobby with white-marble floors inside. I stepped through, and the door closed behind me, cutting off all the noise from the street. I crept toward the clerk standing behind the massive oak counter. As I prowled through the room, I took in my surroundings. There was a restaurant to my right and a bay of elevators to my left, with a hallway disappearing through an archway beyond that. A bellboy sat in a cubby next to the elevator.

The clerk wore an all-black uniform, from his button-up shirt to his jacket, tie, and trousers. It was a severe style, with the only pop of color being a silver-and-blue tie pin. He smiled at me as I stepped up to the counter and cleared my throat. It was a practiced customer service smile that didn't reach his eyes.

"Hi, I was hoping you might be able to help me with something," I said.

"Of course, ma'am. What can I do for you today?"

"I was supposed to meet my friend for dinner, but I can't remember if she said she was staying here or at the Carlton down the street. Could you check?" I smiled as I drummed my fingers on the counter.

He followed my fingers with his eyes for a second before answering. "I am not at liberty to discuss any of our clients, ma'am."

"My phone died, and I don't have another way to reach out to her." I leaned against the counter and gave him my best pity-me look.

"There is a charger bank in the lounge down the hall. While we don't typically let nonguests enter, you can use it for a few minutes if you need," he offered.

"If I give you her name, can you tell me if she's here?"

"As I stated before, I am not at liberty to discuss our clients. Unless you had something else you need, I really should get back to my work," he said, staring pointedly past my shoulder. A couple had gotten off the elevator, and they now stood in line behind me with a pile of suitcases at their feet.

"Her name is Vanessa Bennett. Tall woman. Beautiful smile." I studied his face, looking for a hint of recognition. He didn't give one.

"Ma'am. I cannot discuss our clients. Now, if you wouldn't mind." He closed down, the smile vanishing from his face.

I sighed and pushed myself away from the counter. The couple moved up as I stalked away.

I stepped out onto the street and paused on the sidewalk. *What did I expect? Stupid. Of course they wouldn't reveal who stayed here to some stranger off the street.* From what I had read online, it was almost impossible to reserve a room without knowing the owner. That begged the question—why was a retired model here? Vanessa didn't lead a lavish lifestyle anymore. If she did, she wouldn't have chosen a place like Point Pleasant to settle down. I chewed on my lip as I contemplated my next steps. I'd come too far to fail now. If she stayed here, maybe she went to a restaurant nearby.

I pulled out my phone and tried to search for places that fit her aesthetic. She posted a lot of food photos on her profile. The pictures were of health-conscious foods, which included lots of salads and quinoa rice bowls. Seattle was teeming with choices. Over twenty restaurants within a few blocks of the hotel might fit the bill. If this were Point Pleasant or Spokane, narrowing down the choices would have been much easier. I groaned in frustration and shoved my phone into my pocket. I turned on my heel and almost slammed into the bellboy.

I stumbled back. "Oh my gosh, I didn't see you there."

"No worries." He laughed. "Everything okay there, ma'am?"

He was a young man. There was a soft expression on his face, and he struck me as a romantic at heart. I smiled weakly. A gentler approach might be more helpful. I'd pushed too hard inside. *I need to play my cards right.*

"I'll be okay, I think," I said at last.

Concern flashed in his eyes. "Is there anything I can help you with?"

"Oh, probably not." I flapped my hands to play up my distressed demeanor. "I'm trying to help a friend of mine. Her son is worried about her. She has a history of getting wrapped up in toxic relationships, and now she isn't answering her phone. She hasn't been at home for at least a week. He asked me to check up on her, but I don't have the first clue about what I'm doing. This is one place she likes to stay when she gets swept up in things."

After the first lie, the rest rolled off my tongue. It was

disturbing how easy it was to come up with a cover story. If he poked at it at all, I was sure it would fall apart. But one thing I'd learned over the years of handling claims was that so few people delved into those harder questions. Most people had an instinct to trust, especially when someone's safety was at stake.

He glanced at the door before taking a step forward and lowering his voice. "What does she look like?"

I pulled out my phone and opened up a photo. "Her name is Vanessa. She can be a bit of a diva sometimes. But she's got a good heart, you know?"

He studied the picture for a moment. "She looks familiar."

There was a tingle in the back of my mind. It was a sensation I'd felt my entire life when I talked to someone who was holding back. I'd always thought it was my instincts, but now I knew it was a part of my magic urging me onward.

"Really? All I want is to find her to make sure she hasn't gotten in over her head again. With the last guy, it got really bad. He could have put her in the hospital."

His eyes flicked between the photo and my hopeful face. He ran his hand through his hair and stepped in closer. "Yeah, she checked in last week. I remember seeing her in the hotel restaurant for a late breakfast most mornings. Other than that, I don't think she left her room."

"So she's been here all week?" I held my breath, waiting for his answer. *If she was here all week, it couldn't have been her who did it.* My mind reeled at the possibility. I was so certain it was her. *If it wasn't her, then who was it?*

"Yep. All week. She checked out last night. She seemed happy. Although"—he looked over his shoulder again to make sure no one could hear him—"I think I saw a ring on her guy's finger. If you know what I'm saying?"

I nodded solemnly. I reached out and gripped his hand. "Thank you."

He smiled back. "You're welcome."

I stepped away and headed toward the parking garage. I yawned. The excitement of the chase was wearing off. Being constantly on alert had worn me down, and now all I wanted was to take a good, long nap. Instead, I had a long commute back home to deal with.

I stopped in my tracks and looked back at the bellboy. I caught him with his hand still on the doorknob. "Is there a decent coffee shop around here? I could use a quick pick-me-up before I hit the road."

"Yeah." He stepped away from the building and gestured up the hill. "There's a great place about a block up. It's under the sushi restaurant, so when you reach that, take the steps next to the red door down. It's the best coffee in all of Seattle."

His directions were easy enough to follow. The café was minimalist in design. It was a small hole-in-the-wall place, but everything inside was sleek and well organized. Along the entrance wall, a bar looked out at the street. People hunched over their laptops, with their coffees quickly cooling by their sides, filled the counter. I got into line and read the menu above the register while I waited. Just like the parking, coffee in here was expensive. I hoped it was worth the price.

I tapped my foot and scanned the room as the line moved slowly. I paused as my eyes swept over a guy ahead of me. *Where do I know him from?* I studied his profile as the line inched forward. *I saw his picture earlier today. He works with Leonard.*

I quickly pulled up Leo's LinkedIn profile and glanced through his information. They worked at the same company and had gone to a few of the same industry events last year. I shuffled forward in the line as I scrolled. They hadn't been to anything together recently, which seemed perfect. I decided to give my acting chops a try again. After ordering my coffee, I stepped to the side and made a big show of looking over at him and looking surprised. I made my way over to where he stood waiting for his own drink.

I smiled. "Paul! Long time no see. How have you been?"

He smiled, trying to cover the look of confusion. "Good, good. It has been a while. Remind me again—when did we last see each other? It's been so long."

"The Hamilton and Gray fundraiser. We met briefly. I rarely get invited to those sorts of things, working in facilities and all. But I went to high school with Leonard, so he got me added to the list."

"Right. Right. Yeah. I remember that event. I felt so bad for the AV people. If it could go wrong, it did." He laughed.

I joined in. "Yeah. I almost wonder if Leonard thought I was bad luck or something. It's probably why he hasn't invited me back since. I haven't heard from him in a few weeks. How has it been working with him? He still lost in the clouds, chasing the next creative dream?"

His look turned somber. "He's unfortunately no longer with the company. I miss working with the guy, though."

"Paul!" the barista called out.

He looked over. "It was great catching up. I'll see you around."

"Sure thing."

No longer with the company? Now that could be a motive. Leonard was Jessica's closest living relative. From what I understood, he stood to inherit everything when she died. *If he had no job and still had bills to pay, he could have done it for the money.* It would explain why he wanted to rush through everything. It definitely gave me something to think about— and questions to ask when I'd see him tomorrow to go over the photos I took of her place. My heart skipped a beat. I really was doing this. I was investigating a murder.

"Dani!" the barista shouted. I grabbed my drink and left.

The entire ferry ride back, I stared blankly out the window at the water. While I had not actively used my magic, I had still relied on it to guide me. If the bellboy hadn't been there, going the old-fashioned investigative route would have gotten me nowhere. It was only when I mixed the two that I got the answers I needed. I settled back into the booth, closing my eyes. *I need to read the journal again. In the morning, I will have to talk to Leonard, and I'll only have one crack at the conversation. I can't risk screwing it up like I did with the clerk.*

When the ferry arrived back on Whidbey, I drove straight home. I paced around the living room quickly, touching the couch, floor, and any other object I would come into contact with while I worked. With each item I touched, emotions flashed through me but faded quickly. I touched everything a second time. Now everything had an excited, almost hopeful aura. Smiling, I dropped to the floor and pulled out my grandmother's journal. I counted backward from ten in my head before opening it.

My grandmother had filled page after page with spells and magical theory. Almost all of the spells had to do with memory recall or expanding the senses in some way. Tucked away on the last few pages were a few spells that expanded beyond that. But even they involved memories, emotions, and the senses. It was all experiential, and the theory behind them was overwhelming. The first page was filled with an explanation on the importance of the caster's intention, and it was repeated in some form or other throughout the book.

Magic is powerful but also shapeless and raw. Only through our force of will does it become something that can be guided. You can use it to do almost anything, so long as your intention is clear and your will is strong enough.

If they are not, magic is also blind and uncaring. It is a force of nature. It can consume and destroy as easily as it can protect and save in trained hands. To the untrained, the scared, and the frightened, it can manifest as your worst nightmare.

The spells within these pages have been passed down through the generations of our family. Their structure helps us focus our intention and allows us to shape magic in a consistent manner. In your early days, do not stray from these guides. Always hold your intention clearly in your mind. Do not waver. If you are uncertain, your magic will feel it. Do not attempt a single spell unless you are sure.

The pressure of my grandmother's expectations and warning weighed heavy on me. *Am I making a mistake trying to use magic? I don't have to use it. But... if it's needed... shouldn't I know just in case?*

I read through the night. Almost eight pages of the journal were dedicated to experiencing a memory of an object. I was on my second reread of the section when I realized why I hadn't gotten much off the ceramic shard at Jessica's house. At the basic levels, I could only experience what the object would have experienced—and the shard didn't have eyes. To see from an object's perspective, it either had to have a camera or an image of an eye. The shard only had flowers.

Around two in the morning, I found a spell simple enough for me to handle. I reread it again and again, murmuring the words under my breath, until I fell asleep on the couch, my head on the pages. For the first time in a week, I didn't dream. I slept peacefully until the dawn light woke me. I yawned, stretched, and shuffled up to the bedroom to grab a few more hours of sleep before I had to meet Leonard for breakfast.

CHAPTER 13

I arrived at the bistro a few minutes early, but Leonard still beat me there. I watched him through the window. He sat, staring down at his hands. His normally clean face had a few days' worth of stubble across his chin. He looked oddly small in his wrinkled shirt with the buttons crooked. I kept my eyes on him as I pulled out my grandmother's journal and reviewed the spell one last time before getting out of the car. I repeated it in my head as I walked into Eats and Treats, and I slid into the booth across from him. The thought I might be sitting across from a murderer lingered in my mind, making it difficult to focus. I repeated the spell to myself as I waited for the perfect opportunity to use it.

"Hey, Dani." Up close, he looked worse. Bags hung under his bloodshot eyes. He didn't look like a killer, but he might be a talented actor.

"Hey, Leo. You put in your order already?"

"No. I'm not sure if I could eat anything." He sighed and rubbed the bridge of his nose.

"Not even Abby's peach cobbler?" I smiled weakly as my heart raced. The easiest way to make sure the spell worked right, according to my grandma's notes, was if he consumed it. It turned the food or drink into a potion, infusing it with the caster's magic.

He chuckled. "I could probably make some room for that."

"It's on me." I scooted out and walked over to the counter. With each step, I repeated the spell in my head. I fumbled through the order and stepped aside so Abby could help the next person in line. As I waited for the food, I watched him in the booth. He sat with his shoulders slumped. I bit my lip. *How do I start? "Hey, Leonard, what's it like being unemployed? And oh, now that we're on difficult subjects, I'm wondering if you killed Jessica?"* I chuckled at myself. *Think, Dani. Subtle, open-ended questions. I've got this.*

Abby slid the tray of food to me across the counter. She had put an extra scoop of ice cream in each bowl.

"Thanks, Abby," I said, smiling.

I lingered at the counter and tracked her out of the corner of my eye. When she was out of earshot, I bowed my head over the food. While there had been no truth spells in the journal, the spell I had chosen was a close second. It made the target feel safe and trusting. At least, in this version, it did. If I made the food myself and could control the ingredients, I could choose the emotion he felt. I uttered his name to set him as the target of the spell and held the intent in my mind as I murmured the rest of the words. A white light flowed out of my mouth and into the food. *Shoot. Shoot. Shoot. The journal claimed this one was subtle.*

I jerked upright and looked around. The chatter in the bistro didn't change. Everyone sat, focused on their own conversations. No one noticed the light shimmering through the dish. My eyes flicked from person to person. *Am I the only one who can see it?*

I swallowed, gathered up the cobblers, and crossed the room to Leonard. My hands shook as I slid his cobbler in front of him and waited for him to take a bite. He didn't bat an eyelash at the glittering motes of light surrounding his food. He took a bite, closing his eyes in appreciation. Abby's cobblers were delicious. She added a secret blend of spices to the crumble on top, which gave it a sweet smoky flavor that pulled the whole dish together. It didn't seem like the magic impacted the taste at all.

We ate in silence for a few minutes. Once I'd finished my cobbler, I pushed it to the side and watched as Leonard took the last few bites of his.

"I guess I was hungry." He smiled sheepishly.

"When my grandfather passed, I forgot to eat a lot. If my daughter hadn't been there, shoving food into my face every day, I probably wouldn't have eaten for days on end. If it wasn't for this place, I wouldn't be eating much now. First my gran, and now Jess…" I reached across the table and gripped his hand. I squeezed it reassuringly. "How are you holding up?"

"Exhausted. I want all of this to be over. You know?" He clutched at me before coughing, drawing his hand back, and shoving them under the table.

Alarm bells rang in my head. When someone pushed for a quick closure during a claim, it sometimes left me with a hinky feeling. I had that feeling now. *Calm yourself. It's only another minute for the spell to take effect.* I glanced at the clock above the door and counted down. *How will I know when it's active?* I fought the urge to chew on my lip. I had a bad habit of biting my lips when I was thinking or nervous. It was a quirk Leonard was aware of. If he'd killed Jessica, I didn't want to tip my hand. *Relax.*

I reached into my bag and pulled out my camera. "Well, if it makes you feel better, everything at her house looks good. No demo work was needed. In fact, overall, the house is in great condition. There are only a few areas you might want to touch up before putting it onto the market. I took a few shots."

He accepted the camera from me and looked through the pictures. "You've got a good eye."

"Thanks."

He continued to scroll. As he flipped to the last photo, the shimmer from the spell swirled around him. The air glowed for a second before the light settled into his skin. It left him with a slightly incandescent quality. His shoulders relaxed, and he slumped into the booth, a contented sigh escaping his lips.

"So"—I studied him carefully as I spoke—"you must be looking forward to things getting back to normal. When are you headed back to the office?"

He didn't blink at the question. His brow creased, and a frown formed on his face. "I'm not going back to Seattle."

"Oh?"

"Yeah. I'm moving to Austin." He put down the camera and held my gaze. "Just between you and me, I sold my third of the business a few months ago. I've been doing the legwork to set up my own company in Austin. My bid on a house was accepted a few weeks back, and we're supposed to be closing any day now."

"Wow. That's great." *A few weeks? His offer would have been accepted before her death.*

"Yeah. It's been a bit of a whirlwind. But I wanted more artistic control over the games we were making, so it's a good move for me. Our stock was at an all-time high, so I figured, why not now? The sale hasn't been publicly announced yet, though."

I sagged onto the bench and nodded. His words replayed in my head. *"A few weeks ago." "All-time high." Leonard didn't have a motive. He didn't need the money.*

"These are really great, Dani." He picked the camera back up. "Would you mind taking some more once the work's been done? Good photos will really help the house sell."

"Sure." I smiled. "Is there anything else I can help you with?"

"Now that you mention it, I had been planning on putting together a photo wall. Jessica over the years, that sort of thing. I haven't had time to collect the photos yet. You've got such a great eye. Would you mind helping me put something together?"

It would be another chance to get back into the house. In my haste to warn Heather, I hadn't actually gone upstairs. *What if I missed something?* I nodded. "Of course."

"I had planned on asking Heather…"

"Yeah, it's crazy. I can't believe they took her in for questioning," I said.

"I know. They're still holding her for questioning. It's just so unbelievable. Murdered? How could anyone want to hurt Jessica?" He shook his head. The light faded from his skin. As it dimmed, the tension in his shoulders returned.

"I don't know," I whispered.

And I really didn't. Jessica was a sweet soul. It didn't make any sense. I was glad it wasn't Leonard, but now I was left wondering who else it could have been. The only person left on my list was Richard, and I hadn't formally met the guy yet. *Why are they still holding Heather? Do they have more than the tea bag, or is Bob really just worried about the upcoming election?* He had sailed by in the primaries, but a lot could go wrong between now and when the ballots went out in the mail for the election in less than two months.

We chatted for a few more minutes about organizing the memorial. With a question mark hanging over Heather's head, he wasn't sure if he wanted to host it at the café anymore. After a second slice of cobbler, we packed up and left. He trudged away down the street, his hands thrust into his pockets and his head downcast.

Leonard rounded the corner at the end of the block and disappeared from sight. I stood staring after him for a few seconds longer before returning to my car. I slid into the driver's seat and was about to back out of my parking space when I noticed a piece of paper under my windshield wiper. The town was ramping up for their annual cook-off. I popped open the car door and ducked out to grab it, expecting it to be a flier for the event. I tossed it down on the seat next to me and put on my seatbelt. As I clicked it into place, I glanced down at the paper and froze.

It wasn't an advertisement. Instead, it was a plain white envelope. Written across the front was my name.

I picked up the envelope and slipped out a folded piece of notebook paper, the edges jagged. I unfolded it, and a chill traveled down my spine as I read the words written in bold black ink.

Stay out of things that don't involve you. Don't force my hand. You have been warned.

I looked up and searched the street for familiar faces. It was midmorning on a Saturday. Schools were out for the summer, and families had flocked to the area to enjoy the water. Young couples meandered, hand in hand, their heads leaned close together as they whispered to each other. Families walked along the boardwalk down to the pier. Kids yelled and skipped ahead of their parents. Half of them were vaguely familiar, but no one stood out.

The paper itself didn't say anything to me. The lingering emotion on it was purely analytical, as though whoever had written it was checking an item off their to-do list. I shuddered. *Who could be so cold when writing a threatening note?*

I read over the words again. My mind flashed to the note I'd found at Jessica's. I grabbed my bag and pulled it out. I held the notes side by side. It was the same handwriting.

Swallowing, I tucked the threatening note Jessica had received back into my purse. I reread the words of the note that had been left for me. My hands shook, and my mouth went dry. *I haven't found anything yet. Have I? Who is this from?*

I went through the list of people I'd told about the investigation. I'd told Chris, in a way, but it didn't make any sense for him to warn me off. If he was involved, he wouldn't have convinced the sheriff to do an autopsy. *Who else knew? Heather. Olivia. The Retirees.* I hung my head. *The Retirees are gossips. They could have told anyone.* I fumbled with my seatbelt and got out of my car. I stepped out onto the street and dashed back into the bistro.

Abby looked up at me as I flung open the door. Frowning, she came around the counter and took my hand. "Dani? Are you okay? You look like you've seen a ghost."

"Did… did you see anyone messing with my car?"

"No. I didn't. Is everything okay?"

I choked out a sob, shook my head, and dashed out to my car.

Abby followed me out onto the sidewalk. "Dani? What's wrong?"

"I've got to go," I said before diving into my car and slamming the door shut. My mind reeled as I drove home. Every few seconds, I looked at my rearview mirror, half-expecting someone to be behind me. No cars followed me out of town.

I sat trembling behind the steering wheel, crying. The fear and grief were overwhelming. In a few short months, I had lost almost everything. My marriage, followed by my grandmother, my job, and now one of my oldest friends. I stumbled out of the car and walked in a daze up to the house. Once inside, I slumped onto the couch in the living room and cried. *Who could have left that note? Am I safe here?*

I paused and sat up, wiping the tears from my face. I retrieved my bag from the entryway. My hands shook as I rummaged through it for my grandmother's journal. My fingers closed around the leather cover. I pulled it out and flipped through it, searching for the first spell I'd used. I stopped when I found it.

It was a purposeful activation of the Sight. It would help me relive the object's memory. I reread through the different versions. The more complex the spell, the more information I could get and the farther back I could delve. I didn't need to go back far. The note was left on my car less than an hour ago. But the simplest version wouldn't show me much. I wasn't confident enough in my abilities to do a complex version yet, so I settled on the second version of the spell, which would allow me to replay the memory multiple times. My grandmother had noted it was rare to be able to cast a memory recall spell on an object more than once, so if I was worried about missing an important detail, this version was the only way to experience the basics more than once.

I sat cross-legged on the floor, with my grandmother's journal in my lap and the note in front of me. *Intention is everything. I need to know who sent me this note. But doesn't this spell only show the perspective of the object?* I gritted my teeth. *Magic can do anything. If I want it badly enough, it should show me anyway. Right?* I scanned through the directions a few more times until the spell and my intention were solid in my head. I exhaled and shook out my arms.

"Let's see who left you." I whispered the words of the spell. As I spoke, motes of white light spilled out of my fingertips. When I touched the note, the light danced around the page before settling into the paper.

All color faded from the room, and it became dark. I was jostled up and down. *Am I in a pocket?* Fingers, several inches wide, gripped me before shoving me against hot glass. A hard, flat board dropped on my back, pinning me in place. I strained to hear or see anything around me, but everything was hazy and indistinct.

"Show me who left me," I whispered, trying to bend the Sight to my will.

The vision wound back to the fingers gripping me. I fought with it, trying to force it to let me see. *My intention is to see. Show me. If magic can do anything, then let me see. Show me. Show me something important!*

New fingers gripped me. I flew through the air and landed on a soft surface. I was gripped again.

Fear. It was my fear.

No. Show me who left the note. I need to see.

Everything swam together. The sensation of jostling, fingers gripping me, hot glass, tumbling through the air, and landing all overlapped. I swayed in place, and my stomach convulsed as dizziness overwhelmed me. I lurched forward and vomited on the floor. The motes of light faded.

The spell worked, but I couldn't force it to go outside the parameters my grandmother had laid down. *Was my intention not firm enough in my head? No... but I doubted myself.* I wiped my mouth. *I had the rules in the back of my mind, and I've never been good at breaking the rules. And to be fair, my magic did show me what was important. The last important emotion. Mine.*

I whimpered as I slumped against the couch. I pulled my knees up to my chest and hugged them. Even with magic, I was still in the dark. I didn't know who I could trust. Until I did, it wasn't safe to go back to Jessica's house. Someone had warned her, then they'd killed her.

Is someone going to kill me next?

CHAPTER 14

The dream, the notes, and the fear of the unknown played on repeat, distracting me for the rest of the weekend and into Monday. *Have I missed something? Nothing I've found seems useful. What are they warning me away from? Were they spooked by the act of me investigating? I did manage to get the sheriff involved.*

It seemed like an overreaction. But then again, murder seemed like an overreaction to me. I couldn't imagine wanting to kill someone, even in a rage. But this person didn't just murder Jessica—they'd planned it out. It wasn't a rash decision. It was done with purpose. They'd taken the time to acquire hemlock, fashion it into a teabag, and worm its way into Jessica's hands.

I didn't want to be alone, so I dragged myself out of bed and went into the office to review the lists Olivia had put together for me. I had barely read through the first of the folders by lunchtime.

"Go. Eat." Olivia tapped me on my forehead. "You've been in your head all morning. How many more times are you going to file the same paperwork?"

I smiled sheepishly. "I was thinking at least three more times."

She laughed. "For my sanity, can we make it just one? I don't think I can bear listening to you open and close the same drawer one more time."

"All right. I'll go," I said, grabbing my purse. As I shuffled out the front door, I caught my reflection in the glass. My hair was a mess. I combed my fingers through my hair and tied it in a loose knot at the back of my neck. *No wonder Olivia's been staring at me all morning. I look like a madwoman.*

My feet carried me to Abby's out of habit. I lingered outside the door before turning away and continuing up the street to the Slice of Life Diner. While the food wasn't as eclectic as Abby's, it was as delicious. Willow Hargrave, Abby's rival for the best chef in town, ran the diner. They traded trophies back and forth every year. Each win was either a grand victory or a bitter defeat. Abby would give me some serious side-eye if she knew I was eating here. But I didn't have the strength to face her right now, not after how I ran out of her bistro on Saturday.

As I stepped inside, bright, kitschy artwork covering almost every spare inch of space greeted me. The name of the diner was also its theme. Local artists, capturing moments of the town's history, made every single piece. Interspersed between the art were photos of the town and its residents. Above the register was a photo of Betty and Agnes when they were young. They stood arm in arm on the pier, wearing large floppy hats to block out the sun.

The diner specialized in breakfast, pies, and shakes. They served them all day and late into the night. This was the only place in town open past nine o'clock. I grabbed a menu off the counter. The scent of caramelized apples mixed with bacon normally tantalized me. Today, I couldn't figure out what I wanted. No matter how hard I concentrated on reading the menu, only a few words in and my mind would go back to the letter. To Heather. To the mess I had stumbled into. I reread the same menu item six times. After a few minutes, Willow came out from the kitchen and led me to a table. Her mop of wavy blond hair sat piled on top of her head in a messy bun.

"Are you okay, Dani?" she asked.

"This entire week has been a bit much." I stared at my hands. I couldn't bring her into this. She had always been kind to me, but we had never been close. She'd been a few grades above my group of friends, so by the time we were old enough to hang out at the local haunts at night, she was off at culinary school.

"Yeah. This has been a rough year for you. I can't imagine how hard it is to lose a friend right after losing your grandma." She reached across the table to hold my hand.

I squeezed her hand back. "Yeah. And now they're looking at Heather for it too."

Willow gaped at me. "Really? I've been neck-deep preparing for the summer festival all week. I can't believe I missed hearing that. What happened?"

"From what I understand, they suspect her of poisoning Jessica's coffee. She was in there that day…"

She pursed her lips. "Well, that isn't right. Jessica didn't order any drinks that day."

"What?" My head snapped up.

"Yeah. I was in there, trying to convince Heather to reveal her scone recipe before she closed up for the day. Jessica came in to take the measurements for the cat tower. She was a ball of nerves, to be honest. Planning her wedding was running her ragged. She didn't order a thing."

"Are you sure?" I leaned forward, squeezing her hand harder in my excitement.

"Positive. She said she couldn't get her stomach to settle. Do you think I need to tell the sheriff?"

"Yes. Leo said they were still holding her," I said.

"Really? I thought I saw the café open this morning."

I inched forward in my seat until I was pressed against the table. "You saw her this morning?"

She nodded.

She's out. I can see her. I blinked and moved to stand.

"You change your mind about getting something to eat? I can hear your stomach gurgling from here."

"I…" I sat back down. I hadn't eaten in over a day. "Surprise me." I needed to eat, but my brain was already working a mile a minute. If Jessica hadn't ordered a drink, Heather couldn't be the one that poisoned her. I laughed. It felt like a weight had been lifted. *I can see my friend.*

I half jogged, half ran from the diner to the café, my lunch clutched to my chest. Pedestrians turned their heads as I rushed past, murmuring in surprise as I darted between them. As I got closer to the Bizzy Bean, I slowed to a walk. I opened the front door to silence. The café, normally bustling with people, was almost empty. A few of the usual customers were inside. They sat at their tables, whispering to each other.

I approached the counter. Heather stood behind it. Her hair, while usually in a French braid, hung loose, half covering her face. She had bags under her eyes. My mouth became dry, and my throat thickened. I swallowed and forced myself to hold her gaze. She was a gentle soul and one of the kindest individuals I had ever met. I didn't understand how anyone could suspect her.

"Oh, Heather," I said.

Tears leaked out of the corners of her eyes, and I shuffled around the counter. She collapsed into my arms and sobbed. "They thought I did it, Dani. They thought I did it."

"They're grasping at straws," I said, holding her as her tears soaked into my shirt.

"I told them over and over. I didn't do it. I didn't poison her. Jessica didn't order a drink that day, but they didn't believe me. They finally let me go but told me not to leave town. Leave town? Where would I even go?" She clutched to me, her body shaking.

I stroked her hair. "It's going to be okay. Come on. Let's sit down for a moment and catch our breath. Everything is going to be okay."

She pulled away from me and nodded, wiping tears from her eyes. I led her to our table in the back. She continued to sniffle and wipe at her face. She slumped into the booth. I stood over her, looking around the café. All the patrons politely averted their gaze. Their mugs sat next to them, with only the dregs of their coffee remaining. They periodically glared at the busy street, judging everyone who walked by and didn't come in. Heather was loved, and she needed to be reminded of that.

A few feet away, a small white shape moved under one of the empty tables. I smiled and squatted. It was runt of the litter. He was trying to chase after his brothers and sisters but wasn't fast enough. I scooped up him and the mama cat and strode back to the table. I handed the mama to Heather. She smiled and buried her face in the cat's side. Star purred and flopped onto Heather's lap, her paws kneading biscuits in the air.

"I'm so glad you found these guys. Having these cuties around has really been helpful," she said.

"I'm glad," I said. "Any luck finding her owner?"

"No." Heather looked up as she petted the cat. "I meant to put up posters for them, but with everything that's happened, I got distracted."

"Understandable." I sat down across from her and placed the tiny kitten on my chest. He scampered up onto my shoulder. "Things really are going to be okay. I promise. I just came from the diner. Willow told me she remembers Jessica coming in that day, and she knows she didn't order any drinks. She's calling the sheriff's office right now to tell them that."

"She is?" Heather perked up instantly.

"She is."

Heather sighed. Her shoulders slumped, and a small smile played across her lips. "That's honestly the best news I've heard all day."

I smiled as I stroked the kitten. After a minute, he tired and curled up on my shoulder to take a nap. He nestled into my hair and purred. His breath tickled my ear. I tried not to giggle as I readjusted him. "I can't believe they held you all weekend."

"Yeah. Bob kept telling me when a murder is involved, they can extend the time they detain you. I don't know if he really thought I did it or not. He released me a few hours after he gave an interview to the local paper, claiming to have someone in custody."

"That's awful. So you think he did it for the publicity?"

"I hope not, but maybe. Chris was the only one who seemed to believe me. He kept pushing back on detaining me, so Bob pulled him from the case and sent him to investigate graffiti before the reporter arrived."

"Wow. It really has been a crazy few days."

"Tell me about it," she said, "I mean, really. Tell me about it. I can't bear to think about my weekend any longer. How is your investigation going?"

"It's not. It's kind of a mess, to be honest." I filled her in on the case. The only two leads I had led to dead ends. "I must have made someone uncomfortable, though." I looked around to make sure no one was watching. The patrons were still giving us some privacy. I grabbed my purse, pulled out the note I had received, and slid it across the table.

Heather read it, her eyes becoming wide. "Dani, have you shown this to Chris?"

"No," I admitted.

"Why not?" she asked, gaping at me.

Shifting in my seat, I averted my gaze. "I don't know. I was scared. Whoever sent me that note has been watching me. What if Sheriff Wright doesn't believe me and they kill me too?"

"You've got to show someone, Dani. If you don't, how is anyone going to have your back?" she asked.

"I'm showing you, aren't I?" I peered up at her.

"True. But that's not what I meant. If you won't show it to someone who can help, then I will." She frowned and fished for her phone. I reached for the note, but she snatched it away from me.

"Please, just wait a little longer. Taking it to them probably won't help anyone," I begged.

She narrowed her eyes. "Explain."

"Bob's too focused on the election. He probably won't actually take it seriously. The only way I could make him is if I showed him the other note... and then what? He devotes his time trying to prove Jessica was a criminal? She deserves better than that. Chris, the only one who might take me seriously, is off the case. I need more evidence. A solid clue he can't dismiss. I figure either way, I'll still be in the sights of whoever killed her, so I might as well be productive with my time."

She held my gaze for a few seconds before finally nodding.

"Okay," she said as she took a picture of the note. She slid her phone back into her pocket and handed the paper back. "I'll wait, for now. But if you're not going to take it in, I agree you've got to keep investigating. Who else do we have as suspects?"

I bit my lip. "I haven't fully cleared Vanessa yet. It seems like she has a good alibi, but she was close enough she could have slipped out of the hotel, come back here, and committed the murder. I still don't know why she was in Jessica's home that day. She was definitely looking for something."

"All right. And?" Heather took out a pad of paper and started writing notes.

"I don't think Leo is a good suspect anymore, but we might as well leave him on the list for now. He recently sold his third of the business, but it's still possible he needed more capital to start up his own company."

She nodded and jotted it down.

"I haven't looked into Richard yet. I saw them fighting the day she died. Honestly, I think he might be the best suspect right now. I don't know where to start, though. When I went by the station after they brought you in, Bob said Richard had an alibi. But it's poison. Couldn't he have prepped it ahead of time? He wouldn't need to be in the room when it happened."

She added his name to the list, ripped off the piece of paper, and handed it to me. "Do what you do best. Talk to him."

I smiled. I had an excellent excuse to open up the conversation—the memorial for Jessica. "I think I have an idea."

I filled her in on Leo's memorial idea and asked if she had any photos of Jessica she could add to the mix. She disappeared upstairs to check, leaving me alone in the booth with the cats. While I waited, I pulled out my phone and started snapping a few photos. If Heather wanted to find Star's owners, she would need a flier. And if there wasn't one, a good picture would make it a lot more likely for them to be adopted out to furever homes. A picture was worth a thousand words, after all. My phone wasn't as good as my Nikon, but it would do.

When Heather returned, she had a handful of photos.

They went from high school to a few weeks ago, when they had taken silly photos together at the photo booth at the pier. Jessica had such a huge grin on her face. She looked happy. I teared up and tucked away the photos. "I'll get these back to you after the service."

Heather nodded.

"Now, I gotta head out. I need to stop by Jessica's and look for a few more clues. I mean, photos." I grinned.

"Aren't you forgetting something, again?" Heather giggled.

I blushed. The kitten was fast asleep in my hair. I pulled him out and handed him over to Heather.

"It almost seems like you don't want to give him up," she joked.

I smiled. In truth, I didn't. He was a sweet cat. But I couldn't keep him. "I would keep him in a heartbeat if I could. Gotta go."

Olivia would probably be wondering where I had gotten off to. My lunch had taken a lot longer than expected. And I still had to go through all of those files. I dashed out of the café and back to the agency.

My snooping around Jessica's home would have to wait until later. And once I had a few photos in hand, I could ask Leo to set up a meeting with Richard and me to collect a few more.

CHAPTER 15

The rest of the day, I fidgeted at my grandmother's desk as I reviewed the folders. For the first hour, my eyes flicked constantly between the paper and the door. I studied every person who wandered past, wondering if they were the one watching me. After flinching at the chime above the door for the fourth time, I stood and went to the break room to make myself some chamomile tea. *I need to calm down and focus. Get through today. If someone is watching me, then all they will see is me working. And if that is all they are going to see, I might as well be productive.*

The mental pep talk combined with the tea and the repetitive nature of the work settled my nerves. I had never sold a book of business, the industry term for a client list, before and wasn't sure where to begin. My plan to sell it to Olivia hadn't changed, but I had to do it right. After several years working in insurance, I had a few agent contacts in Spokane who could explain the process and how to make it so everyone came out ahead.

After I finished reviewing the last list, I sat, scribbling questions in the margins and updating my to-do list. Olivia packed her things and stopped by my desk. She stood next to me and cleared her throat.

I glanced up at her. "Yes?"

"Did you want to lock up? If not, I'm heading out for the day."

I blinked up at her. "It's four?"

"Fifteen minutes ago."

I glanced at the clock. She wasn't wrong. I ducked my head and grabbed my purse from the floor, my notepad still in hand. I juggled between my purse, notepad, and pen as I tried to cross off a few more items while shuffling across the office to the door.

She laughed. "Everything will still be here tomorrow."

"I know, but I can't help it. You know I'm a completionist." I jotted down, *Call Jack at Neilson and Gray.* As I added the period, I jabbed the pen at the page and capped it with a flourish. "And I'm done."

"All right. Have a good night. I'll see you tomorrow." She half chuckled as she shut the door behind me.

"You too." I waved to Olivia and climbed into my car. I sat behind the wheel, pretending to look at my phone as I studied the area around me out of the corner of my eye. There wasn't a new note on my car. Packs of tourists wandered down the boardwalk, melting ice cream cones in their hands. I slipped my phone into my purse and left.

I drummed my fingers against the steering wheel as I drove, humming along to the radio. When I shared the threatening note with Heather, the weight that had pushed me down all weekend lifted. *She has my back. And now, since she's still under the microscope with the sheriff's department, I have to have hers.*

I parked about a block away from Jessica's house. I sat in my car for a minute, watching the neighborhood. It was quiet. A few cars drove by, but there was no unusual activity. I unlocked the door and paused with my hand on the door handle. *I didn't notice anyone watching me before. Can I use the Sight to check?*

Over the past few days, I had reread the letter and journal so many times I remembered almost every word. While there wasn't a spell to sense danger, there was one that enhanced the senses. I pulled the journal out of my purse and found the spell. It was at the bottom of a page near the back. I scanned through it before balancing the journal on my lap and closing my eyes. I whispered the words under my breath. Halfway through, I stumbled over the words. Pressure built behind my eyes as I restarted the incantation.

Starting over was a mistake.

As the last word left my mouth, my senses exploded. I winced as sunlight pierced my closed lids. I opened them for a second and was almost blinded. I squeezed them shut. Car engines screeched on the roadway, and tires crunching against asphalt two streets over vibrated through my body. The local news blared out of the speakers on a TV in a house to my left. The rough fabric of my jeans chafed painfully against my skin. A bead of sweat slid down my back, leaving an icy trail in its wake. Bracing myself, I opened my eyes.

I squinted against the light and peered around me. Every leaf and blade of grass came into sharp focus. I flinched as a squirrel darted up a tree, its claws scraping the bark. I forced myself to look up and down the street, scanning every window, side street, and parked vehicle for witnesses. No one was watching.

My heightened senses would remain so long as I held onto it with my will. I shook my head, releasing the spell. I gasped as the energy left my body, and the world became muted. With my hands shaking, I pushed open the car door and got out. I plodded up the block up to her place.

It was exactly as I had last left it: the front door locked and secure and the living room in subtle disarray. I headed straight upstairs, almost as if I were following in Vanessa's footsteps, and began opening all the drawers and closets, peering inside at their contents. *It's amazing how much junk we save in our homes. Out of sight and out of mind. Potentially useful items collecting dust. So many things saved for another day. A day that never comes.*

I pulled a few photos off the walls as I moved through the home. Most were recent, but there were a few from when she was a child and her family was still whole. I came to a stop outside her office. *If I was an important clue, where would I be? Would I be lucky enough to find a second clue in here?* Offices were where people kept their important secrets, their dirty laundry hidden away.

I stepped inside. The room was exactly like I'd left it. The books were all in the same position along the shelves. I ran my finger along their spines, reading their titles. No one had been in here since I found the note. *Why didn't the police come in here? Did they find the tea bag and call it a day?*

I walked over to her desk and sat down. It looked out over the empty street. I pulled open drawer after drawer. Each was filled with office supplies, half-filled sketchbooks, and business receipts in neat little file folios. Nothing stood out to me. The sketches were of furniture designs she was working on. She was experimenting with furniture that required no nails. Instead, she would cut the wood precisely so it would hold itself together. The drawings were beautiful in their detail.

I pulled at the handle of the bottom drawer. It slid forward a fraction of an inch and stopped. I jiggled the handle and yanked, willing it to open. It stayed locked.

I stood and lifted every item on the desk. There was nothing tucked away out of sight. I grabbed the cup of pens and dumped it out on the floor. Taped to the bottom was a key. I ripped it out and pushed it into the lock. It fit perfectly. I held my breath as I turned it. The lock clicked open.

Inside were a few file folders. The first folder held her tax returns for the past few years. It paid well to build custom, one-of-a-kind pieces of furniture. I whistled at her income numbers. Jessica had inherited the house from her parents, but even if she hadn't, she would have been able to afford it all on her own. The next folder was dedicated to legal contracts with her clients. The one after that was filled with wedding finances. I glanced through the documents and paused over a confirmation notice. She'd received it the day of her death.

I sat down in the chair and leaned back, staring up at the ceiling. It was a cancellation notice from Paradise Cove Winery. I sat up, pulled out the paper, and read through it again. *She canceled the venue. Did she have cold feet?*

I froze with the paper in hand. I wanted to take it with me, but if it was a clue, the sheriff needed to see it. *Should I take it to him?* Given his dismissive attitude, I might only get one shot at bringing him evidence. I had to be sure. I should leave it. But if someone else broke in and stole it, I could lose the lead.

I pulled out my camera and took a photo of the paper. I slid it back into place before moving on to the last file folder. Inside this one were copies of her life insurance policies, information on her bills and debts, and a copy of her living will.

After her parents died unexpectedly, she went all in on estate planning. She wanted to make sure if she died young, she wouldn't leave people wondering what to do with her things. My heart skipped a beat as I reread the forms. I fumbled with the pages, my palms sweaty. This would make Leonard's life either a lot easier or a lot harder. While unsigned, she had requested a change to her will. Instead of Leo, Richard was going to become her sole beneficiary.

I flipped to the first page. The paperwork had been drafted two weeks before her death. *Why didn't she sign them? Did Leonard know about the change? Did Richard? Who had the bigger motive?* I bit my lip as I looked back through all the documents. It could be Leonard, if he knew it hadn't been finalized. Or Richard, if he assumed it had. He might have assumed he would be dealing with the estate and inheriting everything. I took photos of the important pages, stuffed them back inside the file, locked the drawer, and returned everything to its proper place. I scanned the desk and moved the cup of pens over an inch to where it had been.

What does all this mean? I stood and continued my search of the home. While I didn't find any more clues, I found a few photos and some old negatives in a shoebox in her closet. I boxed up the photos I had collected and left, locking the front door behind me on my way out.

When I turned toward the street, a figure darted out of the gate and disappeared around the corner of the fence. My heart skipped a beat. *Was it the person who left me that note?* Adrenaline surged through my body. *We're in public. Confront them now.* I dropped the box, leaped down the stairs, and sprinted after them. I swung around the gate and skidded to a halt before I slammed into Vanessa. She swallowed when she saw me and smiled.

The radiant smile transformed her face, making it warm and inviting. "Hello there," she said, almost like I hadn't caught her lurking outside my dead friend's house.

"What are you doing here?" I asked, stalking toward her.

"I'm passing by. I live in the neighborhood. And you?" she asked coyly as she backed away from me.

My nostrils flared, and I took another step toward her. My body shook as I balled my hands into fists. *How dare she come here? How dare she disrespect my Jessica?*

"Me?" I bellowed. "Me? I'm working on her memorial. Why are you lurking outside her house?" My voice cracked. I fought back tears.

"I think there's been a misunderstanding. I should go." She backpedaled away from me and tried to flee.

"No." I followed her and grabbed her arm, spinning her toward me. "You need to tell me why you're here."

She wrenched her arm out of my grasp, her eyes wide. "I just wanted it back."

"What back?" I asked.

"The sculpture," she cried.

"What sculpture?" *What on earth was she talking about?*

"Well, don't you know?" she asked sarcastically, rubbing her wrist. "It's the talk of the town. She's had a sculpture confiscated from my yard three times. I won the appeal to have it returned, and she hasn't given it back yet."

"She's dead," I said.

She looked down. "I'm sorry. I just... it's mine. And I wanted it back."

I sighed. *She broke into Jessica's house over a sculpture?*

"What does it look like?" I asked.

"It's glass. About four feet tall. It's an orchid." She straightened and stared down her nose at me.

I'd seen it in Jessica's workshop. It gave me Georgia O'Keefe vibes when I looked at it. I stifled a giggle. This must be the latest battle in their feud—a fight over an orchid sculpture. "I think I saw that in her garage." I pulled out my notepad. "If you give me your number, I'll ask her cousin to call you so you can get it back. I have permission to come in and to collect some items, but I don't know if you can take anything else out right now. It might still be a crime scene."

"Crime scene?" She blinked, clutching at her chest. "What happened? I heard it was heart failure."

"Someone killed her," I said.

She gasped and took another step back. "Murder? Here? But that doesn't make any sense."

I rubbed the bridge of my nose. "Yeah. It doesn't."

"I just... I didn't hurt her. You know that, right? I wanted the sculpture back. That's all."

I held her gaze. Her surprise over this whole thing was

genuine. I knew that with certainty. "I do. What's your phone number, and I'll pass it along?"

She exhaled, releasing the built-up tension in her shoulders. She rattled off her number. "Thank you, and... I'm sorry. About your friend. We didn't get along, but I would never have wanted her dead."

I nodded, blinking back a tear.

She fled down the street. *Now what? I have two leads. Leonard is back on the list of suspects, right under Richard.* We had never spoken. It was time to call Leo to set up a meeting. *Why not handle two birds with one stone?*

I called Leonard as I walked back to the front door to collect the box I'd dropped. He answered on the second ring.

"Hey, Dani," he said, his voice cracking.

"Hey, Leo. You got a minute?" I asked as I crouched to collect the scattered photographs.

"Yeah. I've got time. What's up?"

I told him quickly about the altercation with Vanessa. I did my best to describe the sculpture. He chuckled.

"I'll add her to the list." He sighed. "Thanks for the call, Dani."

"Oh, one more thing." I paused. "I'm working on the photo collection and wondered if Richard might have some good shots of her. Do you think you could arrange a meeting? We haven't formally met. And would you mind being there? I thought we could discuss the details together."

"Good idea. I'll call him."

"Thanks, Leo."

I hung up and returned to my car. Now all I had to do was wait.

CHAPTER 16

Patience had never been one of my strong suits. In claims, there was always another task to do: calls to return, damages to inspect, and invoices to pay. Waiting, without another task to fill the time, was foreign to me. The investigation weighed heavily on my mind as I paced the house, trying to find something to do. Cleaning was too mindless, and I ended up replaying potential conversations in my head. Each conversation became warped into something melancholy. I imagined sitting across from Leo and Richard, the tables turned and them accusing me of disrespecting the dead. As a self-identified fretter, anticipating how interactions were going to go was one of my mainstays. Normally, it was helpful. It let me come into conversations prepared. Today, it left me stuck in an endless loop.

I tried sorting through my grandmother's things. It was too difficult. Each item brought back memories now tinged with regret. I shoved a box of her stuff aside and strode through the house until I reached the living room and found the box of photos I'd collected at Jessica's. I opened the box and pulled out the negatives. A smile crossed my face. It had been a few years since I worked in my darkroom. I scurried downstairs and checked on the developing liquid and other supplies. I had everything I needed to print off a few pictures. With only half a dozen sheets of enlarging paper left, I would have to restock if I wanted to do more. I prepped the room and got to work, looking through the negatives from Jessica's home.

I peered at them through a small magnifying lens to get an idea of the quality of the shots. A lot were out of focus or composed strangely. Of the hundred frames, I selected the best six. The first photo was of Jessica and Richard sitting next to each other on a blanket. She sat, head tipped back, in a moment of frozen laughter. The beach in the background reminded me of Southern California. The next two were of her in college. There was a candid shot of her building furniture and one where she was hand-carving a duck.

The next lot were from high school. There was a sweet photo of her posing for prom, followed by a group shot of her, Marsha, and Peter standing arm in arm, surrounded by trees. It was sunny in the photo. Peter looked almost exactly like he did in his missing-person photo at the sheriff's station. They must have taken it the summer he disappeared.

And lastly, there were two shots of her as a young kid. In one, she was on Santa's lap, crying her eyes out. The other was a multigenerational family photo. Her grandparents sat in the center, with Jessica's family on one side and Leonard's on the other. Jessica and Leonard clung to their grandparents' arms. As children, they'd looked almost identical. The only difference was their hair. Leonard had his white-blond hair cut short, while Jessica had hers in pigtails.

I smiled as I rinsed the last photo and hung it up to dry. Stepping back, I surveyed my work. I still had the touch. The paper had been perfectly exposed. I had cropped the pictures in a way that made everything look idyllic. It captured Jessica.

My phone buzzed in my pocket. I packed up the supplies,

throwing the almost-empty bottles into boxes and tucking them away under the sink. I washed my hands until the chemical smell that clung to my skin was gone. Once dry, I pulled out my phone. A text message from Leonard popped up.

> **LEONARD:**
> Richard will be in town tomorrow. Is a late lunch okay?

> **DANI:**
> A late lunch works fine. Where and when?

> **LEONARD:**
> Eats and Treats at 3?

I bit my lip. The last time I'd seen Abby, I was running out of her bistro. *If we eat there, I might have to explain my behavior in front of them.*

> **DANI:**
> I've been craving French toast all week. Could we do Slice of Life instead?

> **LEONARD:**
> Abby added a crème brûlée French toast to her menu. It's delicious.

I bit my lip, staring at my phone. *Shoot. I'll have to get there early to clear the air. Another thing for the to-do list. At least I'll have a good lunch.* I responded with a single word: *Okay.*

Tomorrow. We were on. In less than a day, I would look into both of their eyes and try to figure out which one of them had killed my friend. Tension returned to my shoulders, traveling up my neck. I rolled them back. They popped in their joints, giving me a second of relief before the tension set back in.

I texted Heather to keep her updated then went upstairs to make myself some tea. While it brewed, I pulled out my grandmother's journal. I stared at it open on the counter. It had only been a week since I'd found out I was a witch, and I was already relying on magic to help me out. I sighed and closed the book. *I can do this on my own.*

I paced the room. *Magic is a skill like any other. Technically, I am doing this on my own.* I hovered over the journal. There were so many options inside. But as my foray into heightening my senses had proved, I wasn't ready for a lot of it. Magic required a strong intention and precision. I opened the journal and flipped through the pages. I paused at the spell I had used on Leonard the last time we'd met.

It had worked, and I knew I could do it. I sat down at the counter, sipping my tea as I reread the spell, and worked on a list of questions. The spell only worked for a few minutes, so I could only ask one or two questions each before the effects wore off. They had to be good ones.

CHAPTER 17

I arrived fifteen minutes early to make sure I beat Richard and Leo to the bistro. I paused in the open doorway, letting in the warm summer air. With it came the sound of seagulls and the scent of salt. It mixed with the lingering aroma from the kitchen of fried apples and melted cheese. It really felt like I was at home. I breathed in, savoring the moment. *I missed this. Spokane never smells this good.*

Abby stood behind the counter. I made eye contact and jerked my head toward one of the booths. I made my way over to it, and she joined me a minute later.

"I wanted to apologize," I said. "The other day when I came in here, I didn't mean to make you worry. It's just been a lot lately. My gran. Jessica. Heather was being held. And when I went out to my car, I found an egg on it. I don't know why, but... my brain jumped to someone egged my car instead of taking a moment to step back and realize I had parked under a tree with a nest in it. I mean, it was too small to be a chicken egg. I don't know what I was thinking."

Abby quickly squeezed my hand. "It's okay. You don't owe me an explanation. I was worried. I'm glad you're all right."

"I'm trying to be."

She squeezed my hand again.

"Today's going to be hard again." I shifted on the bench. "I'm meeting Leo and Richard here to discuss the memorial."

"Oh gosh. Do you need anything?" she asked.

"I think we'll be okay."

Richard stepped inside, the door swinging shut behind him. He looked almost the same as he had the day he'd argued with Jessica outside the bank. Richard wore a light-pink button-up shirt tucked into black slacks. Our gazes met, and recognition flashed in his eyes. He shuffled toward the booth, his head bowed and shoulders slumped.

"Hi, Abby," he said, his voice hoarse. He extended his hand to me. "You must be Dani."

"That's me." We shook; his skin was warm and dry under my fingers. "I'm sorry we couldn't have met under better circumstances. My condolences for your loss."

He nodded and smiled weakly. "Jessica talked about you a lot. It almost feels like I know you already."

"Likewise," I said.

Abby scooted out of the booth and excused herself. She disappeared into the kitchen to begin prepping for the dinner rush. We sat awkwardly, our eyes diverted, hands fidgeting at our sides until Leonard arrived. As he walked through the doors, Richard's shoulders, which had been inching toward his ears, relaxed. My heartbeat, on the other hand, quickened, and my palms became sweaty. *Showtime.*

During the summer months, Abby hired a local student to help take orders. The waitress this year was young and bubbly. She had bright multicolored hair and half stomped to our table, her feet weighted down by black combat boots, with Leo in tow. Leonard wore straight-legged blue jeans with a green polo shirt. Grief hung so heavily in the air it was almost palpable. The waitress dropped the menus on the table, rattled off the daily specials without taking a breath, and scampered away.

"The menu has changed again. Have you tried any of the new items?" I asked Richard.

He shook his head. "I've had a hard time thinking about food. Jess was so indecisive when we ate out. Half the time, I ended up ordering for both of us. And now… now, whenever I think about eating, I wonder what to get her, too, before I stop and it hits me all over again." He shoved the menu away from him.

I wished I knew why, but I couldn't always get a read on people. With some, I knew with certainty when they were holding back. But with others, my instincts didn't seem to work right. With him, I couldn't tell if he was lying. *Is that something I can work on? Is there some sort of magical training I can do to develop the skill more?* I swallowed and set my menu on the table. *Don't be distracted. Focus on the task at hand. I've got to do this.* "Savory or sweet?"

He blinked. "Sweet."

"Actual meal or dessert?"

He cocked his head to one side as he unclenched his hands. "Dessert."

"Hot or cold?"

He pondered for a second before answering. "Cold."

"Surprise or options?"

He smiled sadly. "Surprise."

I nodded. "Leo, do you know what you want?"

"The bacon mac and cheese," he said.

"All right. I'll be right back." I slid out of the booth and walked up to the counter. The waitress glanced up at me, her gaze flicking between me and the booth.

"Can I help you?" she asked, popping her gum.

"I wanted to put in our order. My friend asked me to surprise him," I said, leaning against the counter.

"Yeah." She pulled out her order pad. "What are you guys having?"

"Crème brûlée French toast for me, bacon mac and

cheese for the guy next to me, and a carrot-cake milkshake for my friend."

She slid the order slip into the kitchen. I took a step to the side and peered into the kitchen to watch them prep the food. After the lunchtime rush, customers waited at their tables for their meals. I couldn't hover over the food without someone watching. I waited until they started mixing in the ingredients. Once I could tell which dishes were coming to our table, I whispered the words to the spell, drawing my magic out of me. The spell left my mouth as motes of light, and I blew it gently toward the kitchen, willing it to mingle with the intended food. I smiled as it landed and the food took on a shimmer. I looked around. No one noticed the shimmer. The waitress stood hunched over the counter with her phone in hand, texting. She didn't look up as I went back to the table.

"Food should be out in a few minutes," I said, sliding into the booth.

They both nodded. The table became quiet as we waited. *Wait. Wait for the spell to do its work. Wait.* I forced myself to stay still by staring at my hands folded in my lap.

At last, the waitress dropped the food off at our table. "Can I get you anything else?"

We all shook our heads, and she scurried away.

I poured a drizzle of hot syrup across my French toast before digging in. The clink of forks mingled with contented sighs. Out of the corner of my eye, I watched Leo and Richard eat. As they took their last bites and sips, the glow that had settled over the food seeped into their skin. The spell was ready.

"How are you holding up?" I asked, setting down my fork.

Richard closed his eyes to hold back the tears. "It's all been overwhelming. Every day, there's something else that needs my attention. For the past year, we've been building our lives around each other, and now in less than a week, I've had to pull it all apart. I don't know how I would have done it without Leonard taking care of the arrangements. Not that he had much of a choice."

"Oh?" I asked, prodding them forward.

"I was still her beneficiary," Leo chimed in. "I thought she would have changed that by now, but I guess not."

"She was waiting for the marriage to be finalized before putting in the paperwork. She wanted to sign it with her married name." Richard choked back a sob. *They both knew? If money isn't the motive, then what was? Unless, Leo's sale wasn't going smoothly? Am I grasping here?*

"Is there anything else I can do to help?" Leonard asked.

Richard shook his head. "I don't think so. I have one last thing on my to-do list, and that's calling the venue to cancel."

"The venue?" I asked. *He didn't know?*

"Yeah… I can't believe that's the last thing we talked about. The venue. I was so mad. She had canceled the winery without talking to me about it. I found out when I noticed a down payment for another venue coming out of our wedding fund. I went to the bank, trying to report it as fraud. I thought we found a place we both loved. But she found a place she liked better. They called her in, and she had to clear it up. She was so embarrassed. Our last conversation keeps playing over and over again in my head. How could I let my last words to her be 'If you don't want to marry me, just say so'?" His voice broke, and he blinked back tears.

"Oh, Richard. It was a fight. She knew you loved her." Leo reached across the table and grabbed his hand.

First venue? There was a second place? My thoughts spun in circles, all of my follow-up questions scattered to the wind.

"It's dumb. She wanted the wedding to be perfect, and I was over here thinking she was getting cold feet. I didn't look at the flier she got me until I got on the ferry. And you know what? She was right. Wilton Farms really was a better choice. It would have been perfect." Richard gripped Leo's hand as he spoke. His face crumpled as tears flowed. I had seen a lot of people lie to me before. This wasn't that. This was raw. This was real. It was pure grief. I didn't need my magic to tell me that.

I placed my hand over theirs. I squeezed, letting them know I was there and I understood.

"She knew you loved her," I said, echoing Leo.

Richard slumped into his seat. "When I got the call she was gone, I thought it was a joke at first. And then to find out it was hemlock. Hemlock? I thought it had to be an accident. I kept telling her it wasn't wild carrots that were growing next to her house. I thought it was an accident. But to find out someone did that to her? I just... I don't understand."

"It was growing in her yard?" I asked.

Richard nodded. "Yeah. I finally convinced her to have it taken care of a few weeks back. Leo, weren't you going to help her with it?"

"I did."

Before he could say more, the shimmering light dissipated. My heart sank. He was no longer under the effects of the spell when he continued on. "I'm not much of a gardener myself. So I had Marsha give us a hand with it."

I was so distracted by the dissipating light I couldn't get a read on him either. *Did he ask for help? Or did he harvest some himself? If he was pulled in a few weeks back, that might have been before he closed on his house or the sale of his company went through. He might have had a financial motive back then.*

Richard smiled weakly, cleared his throat, and pulled his hand away. "So, what did you want to talk about?"

I reached into my bag and grabbed the file folder filled with photos of Jessica. "Has Leo told you about his idea for a memorial wall?"

"Yeah. I'm sorry. I haven't been up to looking through my photos yet."

"That's okay. I've asked around for some donations. They

are still coming in, but I think we have an excellent base here."

I slid the photos out and put the first one down on the table. It was her as an infant, in her mother's arms. One by one, I sat the photos down. Each photo was a year or so apart; she grew from infant to small child, to teenager, to college graduate, to who she was now. Who she had been until someone killed her. The last photo was of her with Richard on the beach. He choked back a sob. He reached down and touched her face, his hands shaking.

"I think I need a minute." He stood and ducked outside.

Leonard picked up the last photo and studied her face. "This is great, Dani. It's so much more than I could have asked for. Thank you."

I nodded, blinking back tears of my own.

I felt relieved and lost all at the same time. *Richard didn't do it. Vanessa didn't do it. Heather didn't do it, not that she was an actual suspect. I had cleared Leonard, but maybe not? How am I supposed to figure out who killed her now? Will anyone ever figure it out?* I slumped onto the bench, defeated.

After a few minutes, Richard returned. He slid back into the booth and picked up the picture of them on the beach. "We took this last summer."

"It looks like you took it in SoCal," I said.

He nodded. "Santa Monica. This was not too far from the pier. It was the last day of our vacation. Almost everything went wrong that day. We got on the wrong trolley and realized at the very last second. We jumped off, and she lost her shoe. She got these overpriced, flimsy plastic flip-flops to replace it, but they broke three minutes in." He chuckled. "We spent the entire day hobbling around the city, her shoes breaking every few minutes, for the rest of the day. She was too stubborn to go back to the hotel to pick up another pair."

"Sounds like a terrible day," I said. "You can't tell from the photo."

"No, it was a great day. I mean, it ended up being a great day. She was too tired to continue onto the pier, so we stopped at the beach. Those shoes were cursed or something, because a dog grabbed them and took off. This photo was taken right after. It hit the point it was so ridiculous it became funny. And later that night, on the same beach, I proposed under the stars."

I smiled. It was so Jessica—good following so close to the bad that wonder eclipsed the sour moments.

He wiped a tear from his face and moved onto the next photo. We alternated, each taking a turn to tell a funny story about the photo or the time period it was taken. By the end of the long lunch, we had sorted through all the shots and decided how we wanted to showcase them at the memorial. Photos weren't enough. The stories were what mattered, so we were going to create a wall where everyone would gather so we could share those moments together.

As they left, they promised they would find more photos for the memorial display. As the first speaker, Leonard would tell the first story and pin the first photo on the wall. We would start the service with her as a child and move through her life. We would end with Richard since he was meant to be her future. At the door, I gave Leo and Richard a hug. I watched as they drove off.

I climbed into my car and sat there, my hands poised above the steering wheel. I bit the inside of my lip. Every direction I turned was a dead end. *If I can't figure out the why, then it's time to focus on the how. Hemlock poisoning is an odd way to murder someone. Leo had access.* I pulled out my phone and googled *hemlock poisoning*. My eyes widened at the number of results. There were millions of sites. I tried a few more searches for things like *symptoms of hemlock poisoning* and *what does hemlock taste like*. After my seventh search, I sighed and leaned my head against the steering wheel. The Retirees were right. Anyone using it as a murder weapon would need to know what they were doing. *Does that mean I need to consider all the farmers in the area? Maybe I should wait for the sheriff to figure it out.*

I shook my head and sat back up. While I couldn't figure this out as a novice, there was someone in town who had the expertise to help. Someone Leo claimed to have contacted— Marsha. Two birds with one stone. I could check out Leo's story and at the same time figure out what someone would need to know to use it.

I called Heather to update her, but the line rang for over a minute before going to voicemail. I rubbed at the bridge of my nose as her voicemail greeting played.

"Hey, Heather. It's me, Dani. I just got out of lunch with the boys. It… went well? Richard is off the list, but Leo might be back on it. Call me when you have a chance. I want to bounce some ideas off you. I'm going to make a quick stop by the nursery to see if Marsha knows anything about hemlock. I'm hoping she can point me in the right direction. See you later."

I hung up and started the engine. Smiling, I pulled out of the parking lot.

CHAPTER 18

Marsha's nursery was only five minutes out of town. The sudden change in scenery made it feel so much farther. The roadway went from four lanes to two before it turned off onto a long gravel drive that wound through thick rows of trees. Recent rain had left the road slick, with mud pooling between the stones. The canopy blocked the sun, leaving the narrow drive in perpetual twilight. I slowed, mentally going back through everything I knew. The only stone left unturned was the hemlock.

I pulled to a stop in front of the nursery, which was composed of a series of clear plastic greenhouses flanked by rows of trees. A squat wooden structure sat at its heart. Hydrangeas surrounded the entrance, with small ceramic garden gnomes poking their heads out of the bush. Glass butterflies floated above them on springs. Lining the path were wooden carved rabbits, posed midjump. Perched on the overhang above the doorway was a stone frog with a red painted sign that read Point Pleasant Landscaping hanging underneath. The sign had a cute, almost-cartoon-like tractor on one side. Marsha's grandfather had designed it.

When I climbed out of my car, it struck me how quiet it

was out here. Whidbey Island wasn't large, but you didn't have to go far to feel you were in the middle of nowhere. I breathed in deeply. The air was fresh. The scent of the sea was gone, replaced by wet earth and pine.

I walked up to the wooden shop and entered. A bell above the door jingled. The front room was sparsely furnished but comfortable. Wicker chairs lined the walls, with wooden end tables arranged between them. The far wall was covered in photographs. Marsha smiled out of almost every one of them, her arm wrapped around people from town.

Marsha emerged from the back room. She wiped her hands on a rag and tucked it into a pouch on her utility belt. This Marsha looked very different from the one I saw in town, carting around lawn signs. She was comfortable, wearing jeans and work boots, with her hair pulled back into a messy ponytail, a smudge of dirt on her cheek. I smiled. This Marsha reminded me of the girl I used to know.

"Hey, Dani. What brings you out this way?" She smiled. It was wide and toothy.

I faltered. All of my questions left my mind. I stared at her blankly as a shiver went down my spine despite the room being warm and muggy. I pushed my palm against my stomach, trying to relieve the knot forming in my gut. *Why am I afraid?* Her mannerisms, her smile, looked warm and friendly. But when she spoke, my adrenaline surged, and I forced myself to stay still and smile back. It was like I was staring down a wildcat instead of a friend.

"Everything all right?" She frowned and took a step closer.

"Oh gosh, I don't know where to begin. I started working in my grandmother's yard… my yard… and I realized I don't know a thing about gardening. I thought I was weeding, but I think I started pulling flowers out instead. It's a mess. Dirt was flying. There are holes everywhere, leaves and bulbs scattered around the yard. I'm totally clueless and thought you might be able to help me." My words came out half-jumbled together.

She nodded and leaned her hip against the counter. "Sure. I haven't been to her place in a while. Do you know what's there now? And are you looking at maintaining the same look or changing things up?"

"I want to go back to the classic look, how it looked when I was in high school." My hands shook. I shoved them under my arms, hugging them to my body.

She squinted at me and nodded. "I think I might have some photos of it back in the day."

"I think where I want to start is by clearing the weeds out and fixing the mess I made. I heard there are some dangerous plants around here, though. Poison oak. Hemlock. Things like that. Are there any special things I need to do to handle plants like that?"

"You really haven't gardened much before, have you?" She chuckled.

"No." I laughed.

She stood as still as a statue. I fidgeted, which made her stillness even more pronounced.

"I would be happy to give you a crash course, but it might take a while. You want some tea while we talk?" she asked.

"Sure." I swallowed.

She disappeared into the back room. I exhaled, my shoulders slumping. I shook myself. *Stop being so weird. It's just Marsha.* I paced the room, trying to burn off the excess energy. I paused in front of the wall of photos, my eyes bouncing from face to face. The photos spanned a good forty years. In the earlier ones, the photo's were of Marsha's father. It shifted slowly to Marsha as a kid helping around the store, to more recent photos of her running the business. In every photo, there were smiling faces.

I hovered next to the wall. *Marsha, who was called in to help with hemlock.* The hairs on the back of my neck stood up. I glanced behind me. No one was there. I rubbed a hand down my neck, smoothing them down. *Marsha, who makes her own tea.* I looked from photo to photo, trying to calm my nerves. In each photo, her smile was the same. Practiced. Every single one of them was a show. Every single one of them made me want to flee. *She did it. Marsha killed Jessica. But why? Focus. She doesn't have a reason to think you suspect her yet. There's still time to find a clue to bring to the sheriff.*

My eyes moved past one of the photos twice before I realized it was familiar. I could only make out a shoulder. The rest of the photo was obscured, half-covered by layers of other photos that were added to the wall after it. I slid the top photo to the side and stared down at Jessica's face.

It was like the photo I'd printed yesterday. They wore the same clothes, down to the same hoop earrings and newsboy-style hats. The tree behind them was identical to the tree from the other photo, its branches curving down, with the same magnolia blossom hovering over Jessica's shoulder. It was the same place. The same day. They were maybe thirteen in the photo. Jessica and Marsha stood over the cliffs of Deception Pass, grinning at the camera like they didn't have a care in the world. Except in this photo, it was full of color, the sky bright and blue overhead, and Peter was missing. *Did he take it?*

My fingers shook as I pulled the photo down from the wall. I held my breath as I flipped it over. I knew before I read the handwriting on the back what it would say. In neat, girlish handwriting, there was a date. It was the day Peter disappeared.

I fumbled with my phone. The signal strength flickered between one bar and none. I typed a single word message to Heather: *Help.* I hit Send. The message failed as the bar flickered to zero. The floorboards creaked behind me. I jabbed my finger at the retry button as I turned around.

Marsha stood frozen next to the counter. Her smile was

gone from her face, replaced with a cold, impassive expression. "Find something interesting?" she asked. It came out more like a statement than a question.

"Oh, I was admiring the photos. It's so cool how involved you are in the community." My heart raced. *Peter was there. People searched for him for months. They never came forward. Why? Unless they knew what happened. But what does that have to do with what's going on now?* I tried to picture the page of the spell book I had stashed in my bag. I had used it on Leo twice, but I couldn't recall the words.

"I love this town." She held a cup out to me. "Tea?"

My eyes flicked between her and the cup. My palms became sweaty. I glanced down at my phone screen. The message had failed again. I jabbed Retry once more and shoved it in my purse. "Actually, I think I should head back to the office. I just remembered I have to help Olivia fill out paperwork before the office closes. Silly me."

She took a step toward me and pushed the teacup toward me. "She can wait a little while. It's my special blend. You wouldn't want it to go to waste, would you?"

I swallowed and took a step back, bumping into the wall behind me. The photo I had been holding slipped from my hand and fluttered to the floor.

She looked down at it. "I really should have thrown that away," she said, her voice flat.

The last fragment of friendliness vanished. All that was left was a cold, calculating fury. She dropped the cup and lunged toward me.

I darted to the side and stumbled over the wicker chairs.

She followed me and grabbed my hair, her fingers digging painfully into my scalp.

"Let me go!" I cried out and bucked against her.

After years of working at the nursery, lugging heavy bags of soil and plants around, her arms were stronger. She pushed me down. I flailed against her, clawing at her arms, drawing blood. She didn't wince as she pulled a packet of ground flowers out of her pocket.

"Drinking it would have been so much easier, Dani. But if you insist on doing it the hard way." She snarled.

I stared wide-eyed as the ground-up hemlock came closer and closer to my mouth. She held me in place. I struggled, thrashing about underneath her, but her grip never loosened. My heart raced. She glared at me and wrenched my head back.

This can't be how it ends. I reached blindly for my magic. My grandmother's words played through my head; our power is shaped by our intentions. I delved inside myself and gathered up all my fear, frustration, and anger, and funneled it into a single thought. *Freedom.*

I didn't have time to shape it. I didn't have time for finesse. Or to remember a spell. All I could manage was to shape a crude hammer. But the intention was there. The intention was strong. *Freedom.*

I screamed. Power shot out of me like a hurricane. A wave of red light slammed into Marsha, ripping her away from me. She flew backward into the counter and crumpled to the floor. I stood up and surveyed my surroundings.

The pulse wave shattered the chairs. It blew the windows outward. Glass littered the lawn.

My knees buckled. I almost crumpled to the ground. Every inch of me was heavy. I struggled to raise my head. Marsha crawled to her knees. I yelled wordlessly, pushed myself up with what small amount of adrenaline I had left, and ran.

I slammed hard into the front door, pushing it open. The frame cracked under the strain. I stumbled through it and sprinted down the walkway, skidding to a halt at my car. I jumped inside, threw my purse onto the passenger seat, and hit the power button.

Nothing. My car wouldn't start.

I thrust my hand into my pocket and pulled out my keys. I fumbled with the key fob and pushed it into the ignition. Marsha stepped into the doorway of the shop. She leaned against it and scowled at me. Pure hatred rolled off her. She smirked as I pushed the power button again. *Did she do something to my car?*

"You didn't think I was going to let you leave, did you?" She pushed herself away from the door and limped toward me. "I warned you. If you had stayed out of it, everything would have blown over. A tragedy, unsolved. And now there has to be another one. You brought this on yourself."

My heart leaped into my throat. I threw open the door and darted out of the vehicle. My head swiveled from left to right as I searched for a way out or a way to find help. There was no one else out this far. We were alone. The only thing left for me was to run.

I ran as hard and fast as I could down her long driveway. The crunch of her footsteps followed me. She moved closer, second by second, closing the gap. My lungs burned. A sharp pain stabbed into my side. Tears stung my eyes. I bent my head and propelled myself forward.

Marsha jumped onto my back, slamming me into the ground. I bit my lip. My mouth filled with the taste of copper. I bucked against her. She lost her grip and fell back a step. I crawled forward. My fingers dug into the gravel. She rose behind me and crawled after me.

"I love this town, Dani. I love it. It's mine. You can't take it away from me!" she growled.

She grabbed my leg and pulled me toward her. I slid backward across the ground. Gravel cut into my skin, leaving my arms and stomach raw. I rolled onto my back and kicked at her. She stumbled. I scrambled back. I couldn't stand up before she was on me again.

Her face was red, and the vein on her forehead throbbed. I stared up at her as her hands closed around my neck. I scratched at her, my fingers digging into her fingers. She kept talking, but I couldn't hear her anymore. I reached for my magic, but I was so tired. I couldn't grasp onto it. My heartbeat pulsed in my ears. My vision went black around the edges. Spittle formed at the edge of her mouth, spraying down at me as she shouted at me.

Gravel struck her in the face.

She flinched back. I gasped, taking in oxygen. My throat burned. I blinked, trying to clear the stars from my vision. Something warm trickled down the side of my face. *Am I bleeding?*

Marsha stumbled backward from me. I tried to sit, but my head swam, and I fell backward against the ground. I rolled onto my side and as a pair of legs moved past me. Another set stopped in front of me. I closed my eyes for a second. When I reopened them, my head was in Heather's lap.

I tried to smile at her, but even that slight movement hurt. In the distance, a chickadee called out in its distinctive two-tone trill. It almost sounded like the bird was saying, "Wake up, wake up. It's not time."

My eyelids fluttered. I tried to whisper to it, to tell the bird I was trying, but it was no good. My eyes closed again, and my world went dark.

CHAPTER 19

Every inch of my body ached. *Where am I?* A bitter, artificial lemon scent hung in the air. I cracked my eyes open and stared up at the acoustic-tile ceiling. My head pounded as the fluorescent lights hummed overhead. I pushed myself up, wincing as the abrasions rubbed against the bandages on my arms. I was in a small room with a white curtain on a circular track gathered against the wall. The door was wide and took up almost half of the far wall. I fumbled around on the bed until I found the call button.

I leaned back against the pillows and waited. It didn't take long for a nurse to appear in the doorway. He wore pale-blue scrubs and white sneakers. His hair was short on the sides, with dense twists on the top. His smile lit up his face. "It's good to see you awake."

"Where…" I croaked.

He crossed the room and poured me a small glass of water. "Drink it slowly. You have some nasty contusions on your neck."

I sipped gingerly at the water. My throat was parched, but it still ached as the water went down. "What happened? Did they catch her?"

"Yeah." He took the cup from me and refilled it. "I don't know all the details. But your friends, who have been camped out in the waiting room most of the night, will know a lot more than I do. Are you feeling ready for visitors?"

I nodded.

He disappeared down the hall. Less than a minute later, Heather burst into the room, with Chris only a few steps behind.

"Dani!" Heather flung herself onto my bed, wrapping her arms around me. I winced, and she pulled back. "Sorry. I was so worried."

"Did you catch her?" My voice was still hoarse.

"We did." Chris took a step closer to the bed. "When you're feeling up to it, I'll need to take your statement."

I cleared my throat and took another sip of my water. "I can talk now."

He looked apologetically at Heather. "We're going to need the room."

She fussed over me for a few more minutes before begrudgingly exiting the room. She made me promise to call her the second I got released. Once she was gone, Chris pulled the only chair in the room up next to my bed and took a seat. The notepad looked small in his hands. They shook as he uncapped his pen and started to take notes.

"I found that Leo was supposed to help Jessica remove some hemlock from her property. He said Marsha helped. I wanted to catch him in a lie. I didn't think it was her when I got there. We used to all be friends. I couldn't put my finger on what it was. Something didn't feel right. The way she looked at me. And then she offered to make me tea, and I realized. I tried to turn it down. But she attacked me. I fought her off and ran for my car. I think she tampered with it. I tried to run away. And then… her hands." I gestured to my throat. "If it wasn't for Heather arriving, I don't think I would have made it out of there alive."

"Yeah. You were barely conscious when we got there. I was so scared I was going to lose you."

"How did you guys know I was in trouble? Did my message go through?"

"Heather was worried about you and showed me that note. I wish you would have come to me sooner. With all the work we've been doing together on the campaign, I would have recognized her handwriting anywhere. And then when Heather got your voicemail saying you were going out to the nursery... we got there as quickly as we could."

I reached out and gripped onto his hand. "Thank you for saving me."

He squeezed back.

"What happened to her?"

"We arrested her. She was charged with murder and aggravated assault."

"Wow." I shook my head. "It's so hard to believe. I've known her most of my life. How does someone go from... who she was, to a killer?"

He frowned. "She confessed to everything. She couldn't hide it, not with how we found you guys. But from what she told us, twenty years ago, she, Jessica, and Peter were playing out by the cliffs. She dared him to jump. She didn't think he was going to do it. But he did. He misjudged the distance, fell onto the rocks, and died. It was an accident, but they freaked out. They didn't want to get into trouble. No one knew they were together that day. He was supposed to be out on the pier with some other friends who ditched him to go watch a movie. And you know how kids were back then. They went out to play and came back at the end of the day. When his parents reported him missing, they kept quiet. With Theresa's diagnosis, Jessica wanted to come clean so she could rest in peace. She didn't want his mother dying not knowing the truth. Marsha was convinced it would ruin her husband's reelection, so she took matters into her own hands. She tried to make it look like Jessica died from heart failure like her parents. She broke in that morning to cover it up, but Heather arrived before she had a chance to clean it all and she missed the teabag. And then you pushed us to do an autopsy. Things spiraled. She panicked. It went from one accident, to one homicide... and one assault." He glanced at my throat.

"That's awful." I murmured. *Jessica covered up Peter's death?* A week ago, I wouldn't have been able to imagine carrying a secret that big around with me. But now I could. I was carrying a secret. I was a witch. But my secret wasn't hurting anyone. *Jessica... you wanted to come clean. You didn't want to hurt anyone anymore. Poor Theresa. She probably knew, but to have it confirmed after all these years... Poor Bob...* "How are Bob and Theresa doing?"

"She's barely holding it together. He's taking a few weeks off to spend time with her. He's put me temporarily in charge."

I chuckled. The movement made me wince. "You poor thing. The first murder in Point Pleasant in a decade. I can't imagine the paperwork that's involved."

He smiled and shook his head. "Someone's gotta do it. Might as well be me." He cleared his throat and shifted in his chair. "Your car was towed from the scene by Taylor and Sons. When the doctors release you, I can drive you home if you would like."

I nodded. "Why are you being so nice to me? Didn't Ed get you in the divorce?"

"Never." He squeezed my hand again and stood. "Now, you look like you could use some more rest."

He retreated out of the room. My heart fluttered as I replayed the conversation in my head. *"I was so scared I was going to lose you." "Never." What did he mean by that?* We'd been so close as teenagers, but after I married Ed, he'd disappeared from my life. *Or did I disappear from his?*

I sank into the hospital bed. I smiled as I imagined him picking me up from the hospital. *It's never too late to choose happiness, or to start again.*

CHAPTER 20

The day passed in a blur. I slept for over fourteen hours straight, and after that, I slipped in and out of consciousness as my body tried to heal. I woke up briefly when Olivia visited me. She wore a dressing gown and informed me she was one floor up if I needed company. Her baby boy had been born that morning. His name was Zachary Watts IV. I hadn't realized her husband was the third, but it was a cute tradition. She beamed as she described him to me and how much he loved looking around with his big brown eyes. I fell back to sleep with her hand held in mine.

The next morning, the doctors cleared me, with the caveat that someone would check in on me at least twice a day for the next week. Heather and Abigail were more than willing to agree.

The nurses insisted on wheeling me out in a wheelchair. I tried to argue with them, but I got woozy crossing the room and had to sit down. Chris greeted me at the curb. My heart fluttered, and I couldn't stop myself from grinning as he helped me into the car.

We drove in a companionable silence all the way home.

When we pulled into my driveway, he turned to me. "I've been thinking."

"About?"

"Life is too short. I don't want who I was friends with in high school to affect who I can be friends with now. So I propose a clean slate. Let's start fresh. No Ed. Just you, me, and a new beginning. What do you say?"

"Sounds like a plan."

He smiled sheepishly.

"And as new friends," I said, "why don't we go grab coffee together sometime? You know, when I'm not every color of the rainbow."

"I would like that very much."

My heart fluttered. *Play it cool. Climb out of the car and walk away on a high note.* I reached behind me, groping for the door handle. I fumbled with it. He chuckled and got out. He walked around to my door and held it open for me.

"Thanks for driving me home." I said, blushing, as I stood.

He cleared his throat. "So, how long are you going to be staying in town for?"

"Things are still a little up in the air. But I have to deal with my grandmother's estate. Plus, Olivia had her baby. I was thinking about sticking around for a while to help while she is on maternity leave."

"Oh, and then?"

My mind went back to the word I'd said only moments before. *Home.* I wanted to stay. "I inherited some office space in town. I was thinking about opening up my own insurance adjusting firm."

"You're staying?" He smiled.

I smiled back and winced. When I fell onto the gravel, it'd cut me. I had a few stitches on my cheek.

"Are you sure you're okay?" He reached out and squeezed my hand.

"Yeah." I stared at his hand over mine. I wanted to ask him

to stay for a while, but I didn't want to rush it either. We were in new territory. Friends, with a possible coffee date coming soon. I squeezed his hand back and held his gaze. "I'm much better now."

He helped me to the front door. After he left, I collapsed onto the couch. I lay there, drifting in and out of consciousness, as I waited for Taylor and Sons to arrive with my car. Chris had messaged them when we left the hospital, and they were going to be here any minute with my things. I had been without my phone for days.

I was startled awake by a knock. I pushed myself up from the couch and groaned as I shuffled across the room to the front door. When I opened it, Betty stood on the other side. I blinked at her and glanced behind her to see the tow truck with my vehicle. Betty Taylor. It had been her father's company, and now, it belonged to her younger brother. I didn't realize she was still involved in the business.

"I don't help out much these days," she said, almost like she'd heard my thoughts. "But I promised your grandmother I would keep an eye on you, so I owed it to her to make sure everything got back to you safely." She held out my purse.

I took it from her. My mind was foggy. It was difficult to focus on the words.

There was a twinkle in her eye as she smiled at me. "I would hate for you to lose important things of hers. Now, sleep well. And come find me if you ever want to reminisce. I'm sure there's lots of things I could tell you about your grandmother. I'm sure you have questions." And with that, she turned on her heel and strode down the stairs to her brother's truck.

I opened my purse. My grandmother's journal was sitting on top. Slack-jawed, I stumbled forward to call after her, but the truck was already turning out of my driveway. Betty grinned at me and waved.

Does she know?

I walked back into the house, half in a daze. I slumped onto the couch and pulled out the journal. The energy on it felt different. I wasn't the last person to touch it. There was a subtle feeling of relief that was half-masked by worry. *She knows.* I stared down at the journal in my hands. *Betty knows I'm a witch.*

My phone chirped in the bag. I pulled it out. Betty must have charged it for me, because the battery was still almost full. My daughter had left me dozens of messages while I was in the hospital. My throat was still too sore to talk much. I opened up the messages from my daughter. In the most recent one, she threatened to have her dad drive her here if I didn't call her today. I closed my eyes. *That's the last thing I need. Ed would make it out to be a huge favor.*

DANI:
Hey, sweetie. I'm okay. I'm home now.

I hit Send without thinking about it—the connotation of being home. This was home. Even with everything that had happened since I'd arrived in town, it still felt more like home than Spokane did.

My phone rang in my hand. Grace's smiling face popped up on the screen. I sighed and leaned my head back against the seat cushion.

"Hey, honey." My voice croaked.

"That doesn't sound like you're fine."

"Don't worry. I'll be okay. I'm home now," I said. My words were greeted with silence. "Honey?"

"What do you mean by 'home'? Are you back at your apartment?" she whispered.

"No... I... honey, I'm at my grandmother's house."

"Then why did you call it home?" she asked, sniffling. "Are you staying there?"

I closed my eyes. *How do I tell her the news? I only just*

decided. She starts school in the fall. It's going to be okay. "I'm thinking about it."

"But someone attacked you there!"

"And they've been arrested."

"I was so worried about you," she cried.

"Oh, baby. I know. I know that must have scared you. But really, I'm going to be okay. You didn't leave your trip early, did you?"

"Not yet. I'm still trying to find a ride."

"I sound much worse than I feel," I lied. "Don't cut it short on my account. Enjoy your summer break. It's your last one before college, remember? We can talk more about this when you get back."

"Are you sure?" she asked.

"Positive. Enjoy your trip."

She hesitated before agreeing. "I love you."

"Love you too."

I hung up. I stared at the phone in my hands. While I had promised to talk about it with my daughter some more, my mind was made up. I was staying. I texted Heather, telling her I wanted to adopt Charlie, the runt. I had picked a name for him. There was no turning back.

Her excited response brought a smile to my face. She sent me a photo of him with red text above his face saying, *Adopted!*

I dropped my phone and picked up the leather-bound spell book. I hugged it to myself before flipping it open. My fingers trailed from page to page. Without this, without my grandmother's letter, I wouldn't have been able to escape the first time. Marsha would have killed me before Heather and Chris arrived. Magic helped save me.

I flipped to the end, and my finger snagged on the binding. I traced around it, feeling an edge. The paper had been tucked into the binding, hiding the last page. I tugged at it, pulling the paper loose. In bold print at the bottom of the page was a single sentence. My heart skipped a beat.

1 of 7.

I sat bolt upright.

One of seven? There are more journals out there?

My hand hovered over the letters. I lowered my hand to the page. *How complicated is my family legacy? Are there any other secrets my grandmother hid from me?* I had to know. I muttered the memory recall spell and whispered, "Show me what's important," before touching the words.

Curious to see how Dani and Chris's coffee date unfolds? Stay enchanted with more Williams Witch Mystery adventures! Join our mailing list for exclusive updates and receive 'Foresight and the Fateful Ferry,' a free short story by scanning the QR code below. Go on an adventure with Dani and Chris as they journey into Seattle for a fun day out, and things take a dramatic turn when they stumble upon a dead body on the ferry.

THE NEXT BOOK IN THE SERIES

Ready for the next enchanting adventure? You can find all of Eloise Everhart's books by scanning the QR code below.

In book 2, "Tomes and the Tangled Trail, Dani Williams life in Point Pleasant is busier than ever. With the launch of her claims adjusting business, she's ready to tackle new challenges. Or at least she thought she was.

Soon after Dani arrives at the scene of a devastating house fire, it's discovered that the tenant was murdered. To complicate matters, the local sheriff, no fan of hers, bars her from the scene. With her reputation, and the future of her business, hanging in the balance, she faces a tough choice: comply with the sheriff's orders and lose potential clients, or investigate herself. With her newfound witch powers, she can't resist the allure of solving the murder.

As Dani dives into the case, she receives an unexpected visit from her daughter. She announces that she's moving in, turning Dani's world upside down.

Now, Dani must juggle her investigation, running her

budding business, learning about her newly discovered witch heritage, and being a devoted mom to her teenage daughter. Will Dani's powers be enough to solve the case? Find out in this spellbinding tale of magic, suspense, and the enduring strength of family.

ABOUT THE AUTHOR

Eloise Everhart lives in the Pacific Northwest. Her childhood was marked by voracious reading and tabletop roleplaying games, fueling her lifelong passion for storytelling.

By day, she's a dedicated insurance adjuster. It's a career that has honed her sharp eye for detail and developed her inquisitive mind—a skillset she now seamlessly integrates into her cozy mystery writing.

Beyond her storytelling ardor, Eloise is a devoted wife, sharing her home with a menagerie of rescued cats and dogs who have found their furever home in the Everhart household.

ACKNOWLEDGMENTS

In the journey of bringing this novel to life, I have been fortunate to receive the support and guidance of some incredible individuals. Their contributions have been invaluable and have made this book a reality.

To my editors Alyssa Hall and Stefanie Spangler Buswell, your keen insights and dedication to refining my work have transformed it into something I'm truly proud of. Your expertise has been instrumental in shaping this story.

To my beloved husband, Nate, your unwavering support and belief in me has been my bedrock. Without you, I would not have had the courage to continue through all those rewrites. To my sister, Andrea, your love and wit has put my worried mind at ease too many times to count. To my father, Chas, and my mother, Tammy, you fostering my creativity as a child has helped me shape worlds with my words. I will forever be grateful for the love and support of my family.

A special thanks is in order to someone who, though no longer with us in person, continues to be an enduring presence in my heart and my creative journey. Andrew Henderson, your friendship was a beacon of light that inspired me to embark on this writing adventure. You had a remarkable way of saying, "Come on a journey with me," and with those words, you reignited a spark of creativity within me that I'll forever cherish. Your memory lives on in the stories I create, and I hope to carry on the spirit of adventure that you so beautifully embodied.

Though we can no longer share new journeys in this

world, I am grateful for the path you set me on, and I carry your memory with me as I continue to explore the realms of imagination and storytelling.

Made in United States
Orlando, FL
12 July 2025

62777143R10100